Michael Underwood and The Murder Room

>>> This title is part of The Murder Room, our series dedicated to making available out-of-print or hard-to-find titles by classic crime writers.

Crime fiction has always held up a mirror to society. The Victorians were fascinated by sensational murder and the emerging science of detection; now we are obsessed with the forensic detail of violent death. And no other genre has so captivated and enthralled readers.

Vast troves of classic crime writing have for a long time been unavailable to all but the most dedicated frequenters of second-hand bookshops. The advent of digital publishing means that we are now able to bring you the backlists of a huge range of titles by classic and contemporary crime writers, some of which have been out of print for decades.

From the genteel amateur private eyes of the Golden Age and the femmes fatales of pulp fiction, to the morally ambiguous hard-boiled detectives of mid twentieth-century America and their descendants who walk our twenty-first century streets, The Murder Room has it all. **>>>**

The Murder Room
Where Criminal Minds Meet

themurderroom.com

Michael Underwood (1916–1992)

Michael Underwood (the pseudonym of John Michael Evelyn) was born in Worthing, Sussex and educated at Christ Church College, Oxford. He was called to the Bar in 1939 and served in the British army during World War Two. He returned to work in the Department of Public Prosecutions until his retirement in 1976, and wrote almost 50 crime novels informed by his career in the law. His five series characters include Sergeant Nick Atwell and lawyer Rosa Epton, of whom is was said by the *Washington Post* that she 'outdoes Perry Mason'.

Rosa Epton
A Pinch of Snuff
Crime upon Crime
Double Jeopardy
Goddess of Death
A Party to Murder
Death in Camera
The Hidden Man
Death at Deepwood Grange
The Injudicious Judge
The Uninvited Corpse
Dual Enigma
A Compelling Case
A Dangerous Business
Rosa's Dilemma
The Seeds of Murder
Guilty Conscience

Murder with Malice
Crooked Wood

Standalone titles
A Crime Apart
Shem's Demise
The Silent Liars
Anything But the Truth
Smooth Justice
Victim of Circumstance
A Clear Case of Suicide
The Hand of Fate

Death at Deepwood Grange

Michael Underwood

An Orion book

Copyright © Isobel Mackenzie 1986

The right of Michael Underwood to be identified as the author of this
work has been asserted in accordance with the Copyright, Designs and
Patents Act 1988.

This edition published by
The Orion Publishing Group Ltd
Orion House
5 Upper St Martin's Lane
London WC2H 9EA

An Hachette UK company
A CIP catalogue record for this book is available from the British Library

ISBN 978 1 4719 0471 4

www.orionbooks.co.uk

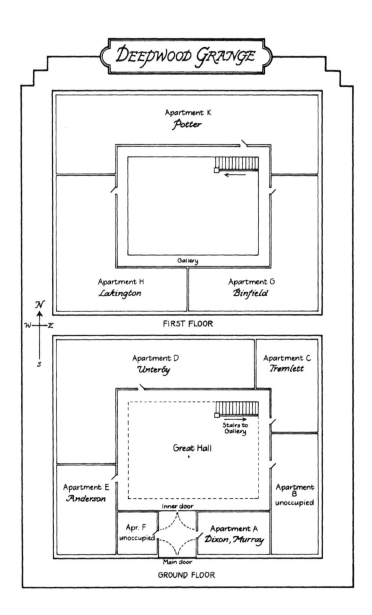

DEEPWOOD GRANGE

Apartment K
Potter

Gallery

Apartment H
Lakington

Apartment G
Binfield

N

W—E

S

FIRST FLOOR

Apartment D
Unterby

Apartment C
Tremlett

Stairs to
Gallery

Great Hall

Apartment E
Anderson

Inner door

Apartment B
unoccupied

Apr. F
unoccupied

Apartment A
Dixon, Murray

Main door

GROUND FLOOR

CHAPTER 1

Though the postmark was blurred and indecipherable, there was something distantly familiar about the handwriting on the envelope, which was bold and confident, even flamboyant.

It was addressed to:

> Rosa Epton, solicitor,
> Snaith & Epton,
> 12 Whitford St,
> London, W6

In the top left-hand corner was written *Strictly Private*, with each word separately underlined twice.

Rosa stared at it with a puzzled frown as she tried to recall why the writing was familiar. In the end she decided the only way to find out was to open it. She did so, however, with a feeling of slight annoyance. It was like skipping to the end of a detective story to discover who dunnit.

The address at the top of the first sheet of paper was *Apartment H, Deepwood Grange, Deepwood, West Sussex*, which only increased her mystification. She not only didn't know anybody living there, but had never even heard of the place. Turning to the last sheet she found the writer's signature and let out a sigh – a sigh that indicated a suspense of judgement until she had read the whole letter.

Your long silent, but ever affectionate godmother, Margaret Lakington, she read. There followed a brief postscript. *If*

1

you remember me at all it will be as Margaret Wiles or Margaret Goodman. Ted Lakington was my third husband.

Aunt Margaret, as Rosa had known her, had dropped out of sight nearly twenty years before. She had been an eccentric friend of her mother's and a totally unsuitable choice for the role of godmother, as Rosa's father, a staid country parson, had been fond of reminding his wife. Rosa recalled having met her only twice. The first time when she was about six years old and the second a few years later. On each occasion her godmother had arrived unheralded at the Herefordshire rectory, departing again some hours later with everyone slightly disorientated by her visit. For a while she had kept in touch by postcards from various parts of the world, but after Rosa's mother had died even the postcards had dried up.

Rosa now turned back to the beginning of the letter. *Dear Rosa,* she read, *I've finally come to rest here and have no intention of uprooting myself again. I've seen enough of the world to last me for the remainder of my days. I've often wondered what had happened to you and then quite by chance I saw your name in a paper, defending in a murder case, and I thought there can't be two Rosa Eptons. It has to be Kate and Alfred Epton's daughter and my god-daughter. Anyway, one of the residents here who is a retired judge looked you up in some legal reference book and here I am writing to you. I would so much enjoy meeting you again. I live on my own and despite three husbands (all now dead) have never had any children, so that it would give me special pleasure to renew contact with a god-daughter.*

This is a beautiful old house which has been converted into flats – or what the agents insist on calling luxury apartments. The residents are a mixed bunch, but we don't have to see more of one another than we wish. After my rackety life I can get on well with most people if I put my mind to it.

We're having a party in the Great Hall, which is common to all of us, in three weeks time – Saturday the 27th – and I'd love it if you'd come down for that weekend. I can promise to make you

2

comfortable and I really do want to get to know you. Please try and come!

As she laid the letter down on her desk, she recalled again her godmother's sudden descents on the peaceful rectory and the exciting smell of perfume that lingered long after her departure, much to her father's disdain. To a child her visits were those of somebody from an exotic world far beyond the surrounding hills.

Why not? Rosa now thought. It could be an amusing weekend. Then, taking the letter with her, she went along to her partner's room.

Robin Snaith gave her an amiable smile as she flopped down in his visitors' chair. He was always quite glad of Rosa's interruptions and still thought the brightest thing he'd ever done was to recognise her potential when she had joined his firm as a clerk. He had not only encouraged her to become qualified, but had later given her a partnership, none of which he had ever regretted.

'Have you ever heard of a place called Deepwood, Robin?' she asked.

'Yes, it's in Sussex, not far from Chichester. There's a Jacobean house there called Deepwood Grange that's been converted into highly expensive flats.'

'Apartments', Rosa corrected him with a grin. 'Don't tell me you know somebody living there?'

'No, but there was an article about the place in one of Susan's glossy magazines and she thought we might invest in one against my retirement. She's always on about moving to Sussex when I retire.' He sighed. 'The fact that I can't afford to retire for at least another twenty years, if then, does nothing to deter her. She goes on studying property advertisements like a Hatton Garden merchant poring over a tray of diamonds. If she'd had her way we'd now own homes in the Cotswolds, on the Costa Blanca and, of course, in Sussex, with a tent pitched outside the bankruptcy court for day to day living. Anyway, what's your interest in Deepwood? Have you acquired a client there?'

'Not a client; a godmother.' As she spoke, she handed him Aunt Margaret's letter.

'I hope you're accepting her invitation', he remarked drily when he'd read it.

'Probably, but why do you hope so?'

'Three husbands, no children and now living at Deepwood Grange, she's obviously looking for someone to whom to leave all her money. How old is she?'

Rosa pulled a face. 'Somewhere in her seventies, I'd think.'

'There you are then! She probably has a Swiss bank account and a trunkload of Krugerrands. You'll be retiring long before me.'

'Be serious for a moment, Robin. Do you think she sounds genuine?'

Robin looked surprised. 'Yes, I'm sure she is. Anyway, go and spend a weekend with her and find out. My bet is that she wants to look you over before changing her will.'

'All I hope is that we'll like one another', Rosa said almost wistfully.

'So you'll definitely accept the invitation?'

'Yes.'

CHAPTER 2

The next day Rosa wrote saying that she was indeed the right Rosa and would be delighted to come for the weekend and looked forward to renewing acquaintance with somebody of whom she had vivid childhood memories. She had written *Dear Aunt Margaret* and by return received a reply which began, *Drop the* aunt *stuff! I've never felt like an aunt and hope I don't look like one, even if I'm old enough to be a great-grandmother!!*

The letter went on to say that she would expect Rosa between six and seven on the Friday evening and that apart from the party on Saturday it would be a quiet weekend. *It'll be lovely to get to know you,* the letter concluded. There was a PS which ran, *I detest the telephone and was relieved that you wrote rather than called me. Let's hope neither of us will be disappointed when we meet!*

It was dark when Rosa reached Deepwood some two and a half weeks later, but there was a clearly illuminated sign at the drive entrance so that she had no problem finding the house. She drove along an avenue of chestnut trees whose leaves lay piled like a dyke wall on either side. Somebody had certainly been busy sweeping, presumably not one of the well-heeled residents.

The house came into view after a couple of hundred yards. Lights showed in many of its windows and a moon revealed a dark crescent of wood on the rising ground behind, which the house seemed to be wearing rather like a stole.

There was a large oval of gravel in front of the house and a huge lantern hung in the portico.

Rosa parked and got out and glanced about her before retrieving her suitcase and locking her car.

'Is that you, Rosa?' a voice suddenly called out.

'Yes.'

A figure emerged from the portico and came toward her.

'I came down a couple of minutes ago when I saw lights coming up the drive. I knew you'd be a punctual person. Welcome to Deepwood Grange!'

Margaret Lakington led the way beneath the portico and through the main entrance door, thence through an inner door into the brightly lit Great Hall.

'My apartment's one floor up', she said, indicating a broad, stone staircase in the farther right-hand corner of the Great Hall. As they walked across she asked Rosa about her journey and talked generally as if they'd known each other for years. More to Rosa's relief than to her surprise, a dramatic reunion was not part of the welcoming process.

As she followed her godmother up the stairs, Rosa took the opportunity of a quick appraisal. She was tall, even willowy, with a lined face and a lot of artfully styled, honey-coloured hair, which Rosa realised with a slight shock was a wig. Her voice was low and somewhat husky, but her eyes and mouth revealed a sharply humorous side to her nature.

The front door to her apartment was off the gallery which ran round the Great Hall at first-floor level.

'How deliciously warm!' Rosa exclaimed gratefully as she stepped inside.

'I've lived too long in warm climates to be able to put up with the cold. That's why I hesitated about coming back to live in England. My last husband was South African and we lived outside Capetown. But when he died two years ago I decided to come home and end my days here. Not that I plan to end them immediately, but at seventy-six each day is a bonus offering.'

'How did you come to find Deepwood Grange?' Rosa asked, as her godmother showed her into the comfortably furnished spare bedroom.

'I first read about the conversion in a South African magazine and then when I came back to look around I made enquiries of the agents and they drove me down here. At that time over half the apartments were still untaken, but now there are only two left. Anyway, I fell in love with this one and made an offer. I moved in about eighteen months ago.' She walked over to a door and opened it. 'Small, but at least it's your own bathroom. I'll leave you to do what you want for a few minutes, then it'll be time for a drink.'

When, a little later, Rosa joined her in the living room, Margaret was already sitting with glass in hand.

'Help yourself, Rosa', she said, pointing to a full complement of bottles and glasses on a table against the wall. 'Are you a whisky person?'

'No, I've never acquired the taste.'

'I don't think young people do drink it much these days.'

'That's largely a question of price.'

'I want a bottle of finest Scotch put in my coffin with me, just in case . . .' Margaret went on, blithely.

Rosa gave a wry smile. 'As long as they don't then cremate you.'

She poured herself a glass of white wine and went on over to the window to look out.

'You'll have to wait until the morning to enjoy the view. There's one spot from where you can just see the tip of the spire of Chichester Cathedral framed between two clumps of trees. But come and sit down and tell me about yourself. . . .'

Several hours later, and after a delicious meal, Rosa indicated that she was ready for bed.

'It's the country air', she remarked. 'I shall sleep like a log.'

'Don't get up until you're ready. I always rise early. It's a lifelong habit.' She gave Rosa an amused smile. 'People always seem surprised to find what a practical person I am. They seem to think that because I lived abroad in countries where there are still servants, I shouldn't be able to boil an egg or sew on a button.'

'I can certainly testify to your cooking after our meal', Rosa said. 'I wish I were a better cook.'

'You're probably being too modest. Anyway, I

7

mustn't keep you from your bed. Tomorrow I'll give you a grand tour and you'll doubtless meet some of the other inhabitants. In any event they'll be unavoidable at the party', she added with a throaty chuckle. Then, giving Rosa a quick kiss on the cheek, she said, 'I'm so glad I got in touch with you, my dear.'

The sun was streaming through the bedroom window when Rosa woke up the next morning. After five minutes of lying there and luxuriating in a sense of delicious indolence she got up and walked across to look out. The scene that met her gaze was as pleasant as the day itself. A herd of milk-chocolate-coloured cows was placidly grazing in a lush meadow. Beyond them three horses were also having a leisurely breakfast.

There was a quiet knock on the door and her godmother appeared.

'Ah, you're up. I'll bring you some breakfast. What do you like?'

'Tea or coffee, whichever's there, and maybe a piece of toast', Rosa said hopefully.

'No egg? No bacon? It's no trouble.'

'I never eat a cooked breakfast at home.'

'But you're not at home. You've all the time in the world for a good old English fry-up.'

'No, just toast will be fine.'

'All right. That won't take long. Go back to bed if you want.'

By the time Margaret returned Rosa had washed and was wrapped in the cashmere dressing gown her sister-in-law had sent her from America.

'It's tea', Margaret said, setting down the tray. 'Also some orange juice. Did you sleep all right?'

'Splendidly. It really is a heavenly view. So peaceful.'

'Except when the bulls are being bullish.' She came over and joined Rosa by the window. 'You can't beat the

English countryside for quiet beauty. Nothing spectacular, but still breathtaking.' As she spoke a tall young man appeared on the gravel path below. 'That's David Anderson, our man of mystery', she remarked.

'He doesn't look a particular man of mystery', Rosa said, following him with her eyes until he disappeared round a corner of the house.

'He has one of the ground-floor apartments and nobody's been able to find out exactly what he does. He's friendly enough, but in an unforthcoming sort of way. He's only been here a few weeks.'

'Probably has private means, but doesn't like to admit to not having to work for a living.'

Margaret shrugged. 'He's out quite a bit, but heaven knows where he goes. He just melts away.'

As far as Rosa was concerned that was the end of David Anderson as a topic of conversation.

'You mentioned in your letter a retired judge who lives here. . . .'

'Yes, Sir Wesley Binfield. He and his wife have the apartment next to this one. He can be a bit pompous and likes to be the centre of attention. He gets quite put out if he doesn't receive proper deference. Not that I give him much! We elected him chairman of our residents' association, and when we have a meeting he tends to treat us like a half-baked jury. His unfortunate wife is a complete doormat. She's quite an intelligent woman – or was once – but after all the mental pummelling she's had from her husband she's given up thinking for herself.'

'I know his name,' Rosa said, 'but he retired about the time I entered the law. He was one of the old school of judges who were unused to public criticism and who could behave like the worst sort of Roman emperor in court.'

'That's Sir Wesley all right. Don't let him browbeat you when you meet him this evening.'

'I'm not easily browbeaten.'

'I didn't think you were.' She made for the door. 'You'll find me in the living room when you're ready to face the world. We'll take a stroll outside and then we might drive into Chichester and have lunch there.'

'Sounds like a nice plan. We can go in my car if you like.'

'I think mine will be more comfortable and I'm a perfectly safe driver. I've got a Mercedes.'

It was a good exit line and Rosa was still smiling when she sat down to eat her breakfast.

It was around half past ten when they set off on a tour of inspection.

'The Great Hall was an open courtyard when the house was originally built in the early seventeenth century', Margaret said, as they came out on to the first-floor gallery. 'It was roofed about a hundred-and-fifty years later when the portico and various other bits were added.'

'Who did the present conversion?' Rosa asked.

'The managing agents are a West End firm called Glass, Merrifield and Co, whose representative, as far as we're concerned, is a hapless young man named Timothy Moxon. He comes down once a week or so and can usually be seen dashing for cover. The actual owner of the property is a Mr Aldo Goran who lives in Geneva. Though he never appears here he maintains a fully furnished apartment over the stables. He's reputed to be a millionaire several times over.'

'Hello there, Margaret', a voice suddenly called out from the Great Hall below.

Margaret let out an exasperated sigh. 'You were going to have to meet her sooner or later,' she hissed into Rosa's ear, 'though I'd hoped it might be later. Her name's Alison Tremlett.'

By the time they reached the bottom of the staircase,

Ms Tremlett was waiting for them with an eager expression.

'You must be Margaret's god-daughter. I'm Alison Tremlett. Margaret's told me all about you.'

Margaret made an impatient sound before saying tartly, 'We can't stop and talk now, Alison. You'll be able to talk to Rosa this evening.' She turned away and led Rosa briskly toward the main door. 'She's a dangerous woman', she went on when they were outside. 'A meddler and as persistent as a wasp in the jam-making season.'

'What's she do?'

'She's a writer. Believe it or not she writes torrid romances which are quite obscene. I'm no prude, but the book she lent me was disgusting.'

'Who reads them?' Rosa asked with interest.

'She claims they're extremely successful and have a therapeutic quality for those in that sort of need.'

Rosa laughed. 'It just shows you can't judge by appearances. She looked to me to suffer from arrested development.'

Alison Tremlett had been wearing a girl's gym slip over a white blouse, with thick purple stockings and a pair of open sandals which had looked as if they might have been a monk's cast-offs. Her faded blonde hair had hung down her back in two plaits.

'When you see her this evening,' Margaret said, 'the plaits will be coiled round her head like strands of old rope. She'll also be festooned with beads and bangles.' After a slight pause she added grimly, 'She's dropped more than a hint that we'll all be appearing within the covers of her next book.'

'I hope she knows the laws of libel.'

'She'll certainly get as close to them as she dares. She told me the other day that she's a bestseller in Iceland and Finland. Presumably she helps to keep out the cold in those parts.'

As they stood with faces turned toward the morning sun, two men came out of the house behind them. Margaret turned her head and smiled.

'Let me introduce my god-daughter', she said in a very different tone from that she had used toward Alison Tremlett. 'Rosa dear, this is John Dixon,' she went on, indicating the taller of the two, 'and this is Desmond Murray. They're two of Deepwood Grange's nicest inhabitants.'

The two men, who looked to be in their mid-thirties, shook Rosa's hand in a welcoming way.

'Delighted to meet you, Miss Epton', John Dixon murmured, while his friend nodded his endorsement. 'We're just going into Chichester, is there anything we can do for you, Margaret?'

'No thank you, John. We're going there ourselves in a few minutes.'

'Why don't we all meet for coffee?' Murray said. 'What about the Cockpit around eleven?'

'Very well, we'll see you there.'

With friendly waves the two men set off toward the row of modern garages which lay about fifty yards from the house in artfully camouflaged surroundings.

'They live in the right-hand apartment as you go through the front door', Margaret said as they disappeared from view.

'Do they work or are they also men of mystery?' Rosa enquired drily.

'They own a restaurant in the area, but it's run by a resident manager. John is an interior designer and Desmond used to be in catering. They obviously made money before they came here and are now enjoying an easier life. They really are an extremely nice couple.' She paused. 'They're clearly gay, but who cares, apart perhaps from Sir Wesley Binfield? Certainly nobody else does.'

'I can imagine they're good copy for Alison Tremlett.'

'She can't keep away from their front door. Incidentally, that's not her nom de guerre. She writes under the name of Griselda Falcon.'

'I've still never heard of her.'

Rosa thoroughly enjoyed her morning. She and Margaret gazed into shop windows and Rosa bought a coloured glass bowl in a craft shop, enchanted by both its shape and its rich emerald hue. The two men were waiting for them when they arrived at the café and seemed to go out of their way to be friendly. John Dixon was especially interested in Rosa's work and quizzed her about the sort of cases she enjoyed most.

'Those with the greatest human interest', she said. 'That's more important to me than the actual crime.'

'I can understand that, but surely all murder cases are fascinating?'

'You'd be surprised how many are extremely humdrum.'

He laughed. 'Humdrum murder', he said, as though savouring the expression. 'Have you ever been involved in any of these big bullion hijack cases?'

'I once had a client who was on the fringe of a large diamond smuggling racket. Fortunately he was so much on the fringe that he got off. As so often in that sort of case the big-timers were never caught. The crime's always planned with the precision of a military operation.'

'So I've read.' After a slight pause he went on, 'In the case you've just mentioned I suppose you learnt quite a bit about diamond smuggling yourself?'

Rosa nodded. 'Lawyers spend their time learning the tricks of other people's trades. In the case of criminal lawyers it's the tricks of their clients' ingenious crimes.'

Shortly afterwards John Dixon paid the bill and they

parted company on the pavement outside, Rosa and Margaret going off to look around the cathedral.

'Aren't they a nice couple?' Margaret said as they walked away. 'And there's nothing camp about them.'

There was something about them, however, that puzzled Rosa, even if she couldn't articulate her feeling.

Desmond Murray, the shorter one, was fair-haired and was clearly the macho one of the two, not that there was anything effeminate about his companion.

Both had been dressed in jeans and T-shirts with Italian made sweaters which Rosa recognised as the season's latest. She hoped she would have a chance to talk to Desmond Murray at the party. There was something about him that induced in her a very distinct tingle of interest. Not that she had any intention of saying this to her godmother – nor to Robin Snaith when she got back to London. She was aware of Robin's wry attitude towards her susceptibility to unsuitable males.

Noise of the party reached their ears as Rosa and Margaret prepared to go down and join the festivities. Rosa was wearing a sage-green dress which she had only recently bought and had brushed her hair until it had a better sheen than any artificial preparation could have given it. Margaret was in royal blue and had on a different wig. It was clearly a case of wigs for occasions and Rosa couldn't help admiring her air of total self-confidence.

As they opened the front door and stepped out on to the gallery, the decibels of sound rose up to engulf them.

'That's Sir Wesley, waiting at the foot of the staircase', Margaret remarked tartly. 'He'll try and monopolise you.'

He was a tall, thin man with a slight stoop, a head of lush, iron-grey hair and a pair of fiercely jutting eyebrows.

'You must be Miss Epton', he said, grasping Rosa's hand as she reached the bottom step.

'She is, and I'll introduce you if you give me half a chance, Wesley', Margaret remarked.

'Very few women solicitors in my day', Sir Wesley went on, ignoring the reproach. 'And certainly none in criminal work. I've never felt that women make good advocates. Isn't their métier, like men shouldn't be ballet dancers in my view. It's something to do with the voice; they have to screech to make themselves heard. Women advocates, that is.'

'Some of the finest voices in the theatre belong to women and they don't screech in order to make themselves heard', Margaret said in a withering tone.

Sir Wesley blinked in surprise, apparently unused to being so flatly contradicted.

'If a woman has to shout in court,' she went on, 'it's probably because the judge is deaf.' She glanced about her. 'What've you done with Sally?'

'Oh, she's here somewhere', Sir Wesley said in a huffed tone. Turning to Rosa, he added, 'I expect your aunt wants to introduce you to other people, Miss Epton, but I hope we have a chance to talk again later.'

'I warned you he could be insufferably pompous', Margaret said as he moved away.

'You certainly knew how to put him down', Rosa replied.

'It's a pity his wife never acquired the art.'

'And how's Mrs Lakington?' a gravelly voice suddenly asked.

'Good evening, Mr Potter. Let me introduce my god-daughter, Miss Epton. She's a lawyer.'

'Pity you weren't around when I used to have my brushes with the law', he said with a friendly leer, to which he added a broad wink.'

'A self-made millionaire', Margaret whispered in

15

Rosa's ear as Mr Potter was led away by a short, stubby woman with an elaborate hair-do. 'That's his wife, Thelma. At least there are no pretensions about Doug Potter. He's as genuine as his bank roll.'

'How does he get on with Sir Wesley?'

'He treats him as a bit of a joke. There's certainly no fraternising between them. As a matter of fact Sir Wesley always seems a bit awkward in his company.'

As Margaret turned to speak to somebody on her other side, Rosa found herself confronted by Alison Tremlett. She was wearing an orange kaftan and had three ropes of brightly coloured beads round her neck.

'You don't mind if I call you Rosa, do you?' she asked breathlessly.

'Of course not.'

'I'm longing to ask you about your work. Tell me, have you ever defended a man on a rape charge?'

'Yes.'

'You have! How did you feel about it?'

'It was just another case', Rosa said nonchalantly. In fact it had been nothing of the sort, but she wasn't going to pander to Alison Tremlett's morbid fancies – less still to those of Griselda Falcon.

'Oh!' her inquisitor said in a disappointed voice, but quickly went on, 'Do you often get involved in sex cases?'

'No.'

'I suppose you don't handle many homosexual cases?' she said in a half-hopeful tone.

'No.'

'What do you feel about pornography? Do you believe it's written by the sick for the perverted?' Ms Tremlett enquired earnestly.

'I imagine those who write it are motivated by profit as much as anything else.'

'I write, you know?'

'So I hear.'

'What did Margaret say about my books?'

'Merely that they weren't her particular cup of tea.'

Alison Tremlett threw back her head and let out a loud laugh, and the beads round her neck did a little dance. 'How tactful and, at the same time, truthful! I doubt whether I have any fans among the residents, though I think the boys would like my books, but they say they don't read novels.'

'Boys?'

'John and Desmond.'

It was at that moment one of the boys joined them. And not a second too soon, Rosa reflected.

'Have you met Desmond?' Alison Tremlett asked.

'Yes, in town this morning.'

'I was about to say to Rosa,' she went on, 'that I've always felt Deepwood Grange would be the perfect setting for a murder. Don't you agree, Desmond?'

'Who are you planning to murder?' he enquired amiably.

'Oh, I'd be much more likely to be the victim than the criminal.'

'So which of us is going to do you in?'

'Oh!' she exclaimed eagerly, as she glanced quickly about her. Before she could go on, however, a man with a goatee beard came up and claimed her attention. She cast Rosa a despairing look, but allowed herself to be led away to meet the bearded one's cousin, who apparently also wrote but hadn't yet had anything published.

It was with distinct relief that Rosa gave her undivided attention to Desmond Murray.

'We didn't get a chance to talk this morning', he said. 'John never let me get a word in.'

'I gather you own a restaurant in the area.'

'Yes. Next time you come down, you and Margaret must be our guests there. She's one of our favourite people here. Actually we bought our apartment simply

17

as an investment.'

'Does that mean you don't intend to stay?'

'We never stay anywhere very long.'

For the party he had changed into a pair of well-cut dark grey trousers, a burgundy red shirt and a casually knotted aquamarine silk scarf round his neck. As Rosa now studied him more closely, she decided that his hair was a not entirely natural colour. It was darker at the roots and she thought it had been artificially bleached. Not that there was anything very remarkable about that these days. A great many men seemed to dye or tint their hair. It had long ceased to be a female prerogative.

'Had you met Sir Wesley Binfield in the course of your work?' he now asked her.

'No, he was before my time.'

'About a hundred years I should think.'

Rosa giggled. 'He didn't have a particularly enviable reputation amongst the sort of people I represent.'

'He certainly doesn't bother to hide his disapproval of John and me.'

'I don't imagine that worries you very much.'

'Not a bit. If he wants to think Sodom has come to Deepwood Grange that's his problem. But we both feel sorry for his wife.' He grinned suddenly. 'I shall never forget the look on his face when he paid a courtesy call on us as chairman of the residents' association and saw our double bed. It was as if the dog had just peed against his leg.'

The front door of the apartment nearest to where they were standing now opened and a young man emerged.

'That's Tim Moxon from the agents in London', Desmond said, observing Rosa's expression. 'That apartment isn't yet occupied and Tim presumably keeps an eye on it. The people who've bought it apparently want a lot of work done before they move in.' As Moxon was about to pass them, Desmond put out a hand to waylay him. 'Come and meet Margaret Lakington's guest. Tim Moxon, Rosa Epton.'

'Oh, how do you do, Miss Epton', he said with an anxious smile.

'You look worried, Tim, what's wrong?' Desmond remarked.

'Nothing's wrong. I just hope everyone's enjoying themselves.' Addressing himself to Rosa, he went on, 'I come down once a week, Miss Epton, and usually try and combine business with pleasure.' He glanced nervously about him as though there might be tigers lurking in the greenery that abounded in large pots around the edge of the Great Hall.

Rosa could imagine that managing a property like Deepwood Grange would not be the easiest of jobs. Its residents could be demanding and difficult. No wonder he wore such an apprehensive air. It would require somebody tough and robust to cope with the likes of Sir Wesley Binfield and Doug Potter, not to mention her own godmother.

'If you'll excuse me, Miss Epton', he murmured and moved away to where David Anderson was standing alone, glass in hand.

'Have you met David Anderson?' Desmond asked, as he watched the two men begin talking.

'No. He's been pointed out to me, but that's all. I gather he's not been here long.'

Desmond nodded with a preoccupied expression. 'Odd sort of place for a lone male to choose to live, wouldn't you say?'

'I hadn't really thought about it', Rosa replied.

There was something in Desmond's manner that advised her to be cautious in what she said. His mood had changed since Tim Moxon had emerged from the unoccupied apartment and spoken to them.

Suddenly, however, he said, 'Why don't we go over

19

and I'll introduce you?'

Rosa found herself following him across the Great Hall to where Anderson was once more standing alone.

'This is Rosa Epton, David. I gather you two haven't yet met. Rosa's Margaret Lakington's weekend guest.'

Anderson shook hands with a grave expression. Gravity appeared to be his hallmark, Rosa decided.

'You're a fairly recent arrival, I gather', she said after a faintly embarrassing silence.

'Yes, and I'm afraid I'm not really a party person. I didn't invite a guest myself.'

'But at least you know all your fellow residents.'

'Yes', he said without particular enthusiasm. 'It's just that I'm not very good at parties.'

'What are you good at?' Rosa asked with a smile in an attempt to inject a bit of spirit into their conversation.

'Yes,' Desmond chimed in, 'tell us what you are good at, David.'

He gave them both a helpless expression. 'I think the answer's nothing. Never have been.'

'Everyone's good at something', Rosa said with another smile.

'Whether or not it can be boasted about is another matter', Desmond added.

They all laughed, but Anderson looked uncomfortable and a moment later excused himself.

'I'm going out to dinner this evening', he said. 'I hadn't intended to stay so long.'

'Poor man!' Rosa remarked as he departed. 'Painful to be as shy as that.'

'Do you really thing he is shy?'

'Don't you?' Rosa asked in surprise.

'Maybe; on the other hand maybe not', Desmond replied, his mind clearly on other matters. 'I think I'd better go and rescue John. He's stuck with Janet Unterby and she can be harder to get away from than a fly-paper. Her husband's a solicitor and they're both on the local council.'

'Where does he practise?'

'In Portsmouth.' He gave Rosa a sudden grin. 'He makes a great point of telling everyone that he doesn't handle crime.'

'Oh!'

'Now, when you're introduced, you'll be able to make his braces twang.'

'Margaret's not mentioned them.'

'I think she finds them both bores.'

'The law seems to be well represented at Deepwood Grange. Anyway, don't let me stop you doing your rescue act.'

'Why don't you come with me?'

'After what you've just told me about Mrs Unterby?'

Desmond grinned in the way that Rosa found attractive. Somehow she couldn't believe he was a hundred per cent homosexual. But was that more hope than conviction? At that moment there was a small commotion in the middle of the room and she glanced across to where Alison Tremlett appeared to have collapsed on the marble floor, where she was making small moaning noises. Those in her immediate vicinity were still looking at her with a mixture of embarrassment and distaste when Doug Potter pushed his way through and bent down to scoop her up as though she were only stuffed with feathers. He carried her over to an ornate chair set against the wall, at which point various other people were stirred into activity with offers of smelling salts and ice cubes and glasses of water. Ms Tremlett opened her eyes and blinked at the surrounding faces.

'I think I must have fainted', she murmured.

'Give us your key, Alison, and I'll take you home', Doug Potter said, helping her to her feet.

Home, in fact, was a mere two yards from where she

21

was sitting, her apartment being next to the unoccupied one from which Tim Moxon had earlier emerged. Thelma Potter opened her front door and Doug, with an arm round Alison's waist, steered her through.

'We'll just make sure she's got everything she needs', Thelma said to those around as she followed them inside.

'I don't think we need wait for a further bulletin', Margaret remarked in Rosa's ear. 'Are you ready to leave?'

Rosa nodded. She had noticed that a number of people had departed, including the Binfields. Margaret said that something had put Sir Wesley in a state of dudgeon and that he'd left early.

Later that evening as they sat, feet up, with bowls of hot soup for supper, Margaret said, 'The catering was quite good, didn't you think? Should have been for what we were paying. John and Desmond made all the arrangements.'

'I thought all the eats, not to mention the drinks, were excellent.'

'I'm not surprised Alison Tremlett passed out. She grabbed at every tray that passed within reach.' She paused. 'I hope you weren't too bored. I saw you having quite an animated talk with Desmond.'

'I enjoyed myself very much', Rosa said, declining to be drawn.

'We're a mixed lot as I said to you, but fortunately we don't have to see more of one another than we want.'

'I liked the way Mr Potter picked up Alison as if she weighed no more than a rag doll. He must be pretty strong for his age.'

'He's as strong as an ox even though he's in his seventies. I saw him shifting packing cases when they moved in and he might have been lifting shoe boxes. Incidentally, you're not leaving before tomorrow evening, are you?'

'I thought I'd start for home around five or six, if that's all right.'

'Splendid! It's only that I've asked the Binfields in for a drink before lunch. He became quite plaintive that he hadn't had an opportunity of talking to you for longer. I thought of inviting Tim Moxon, too, but it wouldn't have been kind as he's terrified of Sir Wesley.'

'He seemed a rather nervy person.'

'Nothing like tough enough for coping with our various demands.' She flashed Rosa a wicked smile. 'Mine, of course, are always reasonable, but not so everyone's. He's fairly adept, however, at simply vanishing when someone's on the warpath. His ultimate line of defence is that he'll have to consult Mr Goran in Geneva. I sometimes wonder if Mr Goran even exists.' Observing Rosa's expression she went on, 'Oh, somebody obviously owns the place. We only have ninety-nine-year leases, but Mr Goran may be another name for Mr Abu Al Khalifa in Kuwait or some other wealthy Arab investing his millions in picturesque England.'

'I can see that Alison Tremlett will never lack copy here', Rosa remarked with a laugh.

'That woman could bring more trouble on herself than she's aware of', Margaret observed tartly.

The Binfields arrived on the dot of twelve the next day. Although the two front doors were less than fifteen yards apart, Lady Binfield disappeared into Margaret's bedroom on arrival to repair the ravages of the journey. It occurred to Rosa that she had been instructed to do so by her husband as he at once sailed into the living room and swept Rosa across to the window seat. When his wife and Margaret appeared, Lady Binfield confirmed the impression by seating herself on a sofa at the other end of the room.

'Margaret and my wife always have so much to talk about', he said airily as he took a sip of his whisky and soda. Rosa, who didn't care for midday drinking, had poured herself a glass of chilled white wine. Even if she didn't have to work that afternoon, she was going to have to drive back to London.

'Of course, when I reached retiring age, I had to go', Sir Wesley now said. 'Not that any of my faculties were impaired. Indeed, I'm as mentally and physically fit now as someone half my age. Just shows up the nonsense of having a fixed retiring age: particularly for High Court judges. Trying to put us on a par with bureaucrats!' He made a dismissive sound. 'I'm still a bencher of my Inn and go up to town for functions, but it's not the same thing and I miss the work.'

'Used you to enjoy trying crime?' Rosa asked, feeling that an occasional prompting question was all that was required of her.

'Provided you know the rules of evidence, it's just a matter of common sense. Never worried me: nor did sentencing. Lot of nonsense talked these days on how to sentence. Seminars for judges and all that sort of thing. Believe me, Miss Epton, criminal justice has never been the same since psychiatrists came on the scene. They pop up in practically every murder case nowadays and seek to fill a jury's head with a lot of half-baked mumbo jumbo. People commit crimes from basic motives like avarice, revenge and naked malice, not because their fathers drank too much or their mother's milk turned sour. I accept that punishment should reflect a measure of retribution. Nothing wrong in that, in my view.'

'What's your feeling about the death penalty?' Rosa asked. As though I didn't know, she thought to herself.

'Take a life, forfeit a life, that's my view. The Home Secretary of the day can be trusted to recommend a reprieve in appropriate cases.' He paused and frowned as

24

a strangely reflective look flitted across his face. 'Though I'm not sure that the prerogative of mercy ought to be left entirely in the hands of one man. Get a too liberal Home Secretary with so-called modern views on penal reform and reprieves could become a matter of course. If the death sentence is ever brought back, I'd like to see a small committee deciding the issue of life and death.'

Doubtless made up of retired hangmen, Rosa reflected and was sorely tempted to say. But Sir Wesley was under full sail and clearly didn't expect to be interrupted.

'I prosecuted and defended quite a few murderers while there was still a death penalty', he went on. 'Some were executed, deservedly in my view; others, for reasons often obscure to me, had their sentences commuted to life imprisonment.' He gave Rosa a sudden accusing stare. 'And we both know how meaningless the term life imprisonment has become.'

To Rosa's relief her godmother chose that moment to come across to where they were sitting.

'You two have been talking shop quite long enough', she said firmly. 'Go and talk to Lady Binfield on the sofa, Rosa.'

'My husband so enjoys reminiscing about the law', Sally Binfield said in a half-apologetic tone as Rosa sat down beside her. 'I think we may have made a mistake leaving London when he retired, but he'd always wanted to live in West Sussex. But somehow he's become a shadow of his old self.'

Some shadow, Rosa felt inclined to observe.

'He won't admit it, but he's unsettled here', Lady Binfield went on in a tone of resigned sadness. 'Something's on his mind. . . .' She glanced quickly about her like a woman walking alone down a dark lane at night. 'Why am I burdening you with my thoughts? But sometimes it's easier to talk to a stranger, especially one with a sympathetic face. We're both so fond of your

25

godmother', she hurried on. 'Such a practical and sensible person. My husband always enjoys talking to her. He says she has a very independent mind for a woman.'

That was something Lady Binfield had long since lost, according to Margaret. She could almost be a case for the psychiatrists her husband held in such contempt.

After the Binfields had departed, Rosa mentioned the worries Sally Binfield had expressed about her husband, and Margaret let out a derisive snort.

'He has the skin of a rhinoceros. She fusses around him and all she gets in return are bouts of emotional blackmail. It's quite sickening. And yet he can be stimulating company when he's not holding forth, while I find her constant self-effacement totally exasperating. She manages to dry up my well of compassion.'

'I wonder what they're like when they're alone', Rosa remarked. 'It could be that she asserts herself and puts him in his place.'

'I very much doubt it. Do you know what he had the cheek to say to me after he'd been talking to you? That he had something he might want you to investigate on his behalf and that he'd been impressed by your intelligence.' She handed Rosa a sandwich and said with a sudden gleeful smile, 'I made these smoked-salmon sandwiches for all of us, but Wesley made me so cross the way he monopolised you that I decided to keep them for our lunch after they'd gone.'

'I'm so glad', Rosa said, helping herself to two.

CHAPTER 3

Rosa had enjoyed her weekend. She liked her god-mother's forthright manner and was glad that they had rediscovered one another. The success of her visit could be measured by the fact that it obviously never occurred to either of them they wouldn't now continue to keep in touch. For Rosa, both of whose parents were dead and whose only brother lived in America, Margaret Laking-ton had been a find.

The next morning Robin Snaith listened with an amused expression while Rosa gave him a lively account of her visit.

'Fancy old Binfield still being alive', he remarked. 'I thought he'd died years ago.'

'Far from it. He now lords it over the residents of Deepwood Grange.'

'I used to go and sit in his court when I was a student. He was a fairly new judge then, but he was always good spectator value. He never bothered to hide his displeasure when a jury failed to return the verdict he wanted.'

'Which was presumably always one of guilty?'

'Of course. Anyway it's good news that your god-mother stands up to him, though I'm not surprised to hear he has a browbeaten wife.'

The phone on Robin's desk rang and he reached for the receiver.

'It's for you', he said, handing it to Rosa. 'A call from West Brompton police station.'

'Miss Epton?' a voice said. 'This is Detective Sergeant

27

Grierson. We have an old friend of yours here, Mickey Rogers. He's coming up in court this morning and would like you to be there.'

'What's he charged with?'

'Handling stolen property, to wit a diamond ring. An extremely valuable one', Sergeant Grierson added complacently.

'How long's he been in custody?'

'We got him out of his bed yesterday morning and he's been our guest since then.'

'All right, tell him I'll be along.'

'I'll do that, Miss Epton. He'll be pleased to know we've been able to contact you.'

'What was that all about?' Robin asked when Rosa put the receiver down. As she finished telling him, he said, 'The police love nothing better than arresting someone over the weekend. It gives them more time to extract a confession and it relieves the boredom of a Sunday on duty.'

'Sergeant Grierson certainly sounded pleased with himself, which doesn't augur well for Mickey Rogers.'

'Who exactly is Mickey Rogers?'

'Curiously enough he came to mind when I was at Deepwood. I happened to tell someone about that diamond smuggling case I was involved in. Mickey Rogers was the chap I got off.'

'No wonder he wants you again.'

'It doesn't sound as if he'll be as lucky this time.' She glanced at her watch. 'I suppose I'd better get to court and find out the score.'

'It's all a 'orrible mistake, Miss Epton', Mickey said when Rosa saw him an hour later. 'I was just minding the ring for a friend. I never knew it was 'ot or I wouldn't 'ave touched it with asbestos gloves.'

'What's the name of the friend, Mickey?' Rosa asked.

'John.'

'Not John Smith?'

'No, it's not like that at all, Miss Epton. 'Is name really is John.'

'John what?'

'I can never remember 'is other name. It's foreign-like.'

'Where does he live?'

'In Fulham.'

'His address, Mickey? His address?'

'I've never been to 'is 'ome, Miss Epton. But 'e does exist, I promise you.'

'Why'd he want you to look after this ring for him?'

''E thought it'd be safer that way as 'e was moving around.'

'Do you know where he got it from? And don't say it was his grandmother's!'

Mickey shook his head in sad reproach. 'You don't seem to believe me, Miss Epton.'

'It's my job to be sceptical. Anyway, what's the supposed value of the ring?'

'About eighty thou.'

'Not something you'd get in a Christmas cracker!' Rosa observed, sardonically. She sighed. 'I suppose you want me to try and get you bail, not that I hold out much hope. I imagine the police have further enquiries to make and will want you tucked up inside while they do so.'

'I must 'ave bail, Miss Epton', he said desperately. 'My girl-friend's going to 'ave a baby. She'll 'ave a miscarriage if I'm not there to look after her. She'll fret, you see.'

'Your girl-friend? You had a wife last time I saw you.'

'She went off with a bloke who was on that diamond job.'

29

Rosa recalled that a heist had preceded the smuggling operation. So far as she knew the police had never identified all the people involved, which presumably included the one with whom Mickey's wife had later decamped. Discretion seemed to preclude further questions on the subject.

In the normal course of events Rosa would have had a word with the officer in charge of the case before speaking to her client, but Sergeant Grierson wasn't at court when she arrived and so she had immediately sought out Mickey Rogers.

'The case obviously won't go ahead today,' she now went on, 'so bail will be the only matter the magistrate has to decide.'

'I got to 'ave bail, Miss Epton', he said in the same urgent tone.

'I'll do my best, but don't bank on it.'

'But even murderers get bail these days.'

'Only rarely.'

'It'll be diabolical if they keep me inside just for minding something for a friend.'

Rosa decided it would be a waste of breath to point out the flaws in this innocent assertion. Instead, saying that she would see him shortly in court she went off in search of Sergeant Grierson.

He was standing talking to another officer in a corner of the crowded jailer's office. Not for the first time, Rosa reflected that the jailer at a busy magistrates' court required special qualities. Amongst them were infinite patience, total unflappability, speed of thought and a good, strong voice. The present incumbent seemed especially well endowed, as he was dealing with several matters at the same time, including the identification to Rosa of Detective Sergeant Grierson.

'I'm Rosa Epton', Rosa said as she approached him. 'I've had a word with my client, but I'd be glad if you'd tell me a bit more about the charge.'

'What would you like to know?'

'Is the ring really worth eighty thousand pounds?'

'That's what it's insured for.'

'Who does it belong to?'

'An Egyptian lady named Mrs Fatima Osman, who has a flat behind Harrods.' He gave Rosa a slightly amused look. 'Shall I go on?'

'Please do.'

'Mrs Osman found the ring missing last Thursday evening when she went to put it on and immediately notified the police. She suspected it had been taken by her maid who was under notice to leave that day. The maid was Portuguese, but she had an English boyfriend.'

'Who had a flat in Fulham?'

'As a matter of fact, yes.'

'What's his name?'

'I'm not at liberty to disclose that.'

'Is it a foreign-sounding name?'

'Could be.'

'Are he and the maid being charged?'

'We still have a great many further enquiries to make.'

'Now for the sixty four thousand dollar question: what led you to my client?'

'We had a tip-off.'

'Any point in my asking you the source?'

'None.'

'It looks to me as if he may have been framed', Rosa remarked with one eyebrow quizzically raised.

'Mickey's never chosen his friends very carefully', Sergeant Grierson retorted with a smug grin.

'What's the position about bail?' Rosa asked after a pause.

'The police have no objection to bail, provided there are suitable sureties.'

Rosa fought to hide her surprise while Sergeant

Grierson permitted himself a small twitch of amusement.

'Was he aware that you wouldn't be opposing bail?' she asked in a tone of faint suspicion.

'Not from me. So you can take the kudos.'

It took all of three minutes for Mickey Rogers to be remanded on bail for three weeks and to be granted legal aid. He was overjoyed at finding himself free.

'You were wonderful, Miss Epton', he said happily.

'I was pushing at an already open door', Rosa replied drily.

She was sure the police had some ulterior motive in their decision not to oppose bail. It was certainly no quixotic act of kindness on their part: more a matter of deviousness matching deviousness.

'If you take my advice,' she went on, 'you'll keep a low profile for the next three weeks. Watch your step all the time.'

'Don't worry, Miss Epton, I will. And if there's anything in the world I can do for you, you only 'ave to ask.'

Rosa smiled. 'I'll remember that. Meanwhile phone my office and make an appointment. I'll need to know much more about the case before we return to court.'

It was her guess that Mickey had been given the ring to dispose of. She recalled from the previous case that he had shown more than an amateur's knowledge in the illicit trafficking of diamonds. It had been his good fortune that the evidence had been insufficient to secure his conviction.

Anyway, she could forget him for the time being and give her mind to more immediate matters.

It was about ten days later that Rosa received another letter from her godmother.

Dear Rosa, (it read), *I have to come to town next Monday and shall be so pleased if we can meet for lunch. What about Le Jardin*

En Eté in Kensington High Street which wouldn't be too far from your office?

You remember David Anderson, our man of mystery? Well, he's lived up to his reputation by disappearing. Nothing has been seen of him for six days and nobody seems to know where he is. It wasn't until the milk bottles began to accumulate outside his front door that speculation began. Tim Moxon has been down here and showing signs of nervous disintegration.

Sir Wesley has again said that he may ask you to undertake some assignment for him. I do nothing to encourage him to tell me what it's all about.

Do hope we can meet on Monday.
                    Yours affectionately,
                    Margaret Lakington.

Although Rosa had a case in court on the morning in question, she was confident it would be finished by twelve and that she would be able to keep the lunch appointment. If something came up for the afternoon, she would have to do a bit of juggling, something at which she had had a lot of practice.

It was exactly half past twelve when she arrived at the restaurant to find her godmother sitting at their table with a drink in front of her. She was dressed in a variety of soft browns, including a dark brown velvet beret which she wore at a becoming angle. She looked extremely elegant.

'Forgive me for starting without you,' she said, 'but I needed a drink.'

'Have you had an exhausting morning?' Rosa asked sympathetically.

'Worse than that', she said in her grainy voice. 'David Anderson was found dead just before I left this morning.'

'Oh, what a terrible shock! I am sorry. He seemed a pleasant young man. What happened?'

'His body was found lodged up a chimney in that unoccupied ground-floor apartment. There was a plastic

33

bag over his head. It had been taped tightly round his neck.'

'How awful! Who found him?'

'Some workmen who came to examine the chimney with a view to installing a gas fire. They found his body on a ledge a little way up.' Drinks arrived, including a replenished glass for Margaret. 'I can't tell you the confusion when I left. Tim Moxon was running round like a demented hen and Sir Wesley had assumed the air of a visiting deity. Alison Tremlett, of course, was behaving as excitedly as a child on Christmas morning. I decided that if I didn't get away quickly, I'd probably be kept hanging around all day while the police took over the house. I just told John and Desmond that I was coming up to town for the day and would be back this evening if anyone wanted to know where I was.'

'I wonder how long the body had been there?' Rosa said thoughtfully.

'Such an undignified way to die!' Margaret exclaimed with feeling.

'Presumably you'll now find out exactly what he did. His air of mystery will be peeled off.'

Margaret finished her drink. 'The most depressing aspect is that for days, if not weeks, we'll have the police tramping in and out and asking endless questions.'

'Not if they make an early arrest.'

'Whoever stuck his body up the chimney had no intention of being quickly arrested!'

'Do you have any theories as to who might have done it?' Rosa asked.

'Everything points to it being an inside job', Margaret said matter-of-factly.

Rosa felt this was unnecessarily melodramatic. After all the body had only been discovered that morning and it was therefore far too soon to draw such a conclusion. Just because it had been found in one of the apartments didn't mean he'd been killed by a fellow resident. There were all sorts of questions to be answered before that conclusion could be reached. For example, who possessed keys to the unoccupied apartment?

'Did you drive up?' Rosa asked, laying her thoughts aside for the moment.

'No. I left my car at the station and came up by train. I hate driving in London and seem to spend all my time looking for somewhere to park.'

'If you like, I'll drive you back this evening', Rosa said after a pause. 'I could give you moral support if the police want to interview you.'

'Oh, Rosa, that would be kind! And of course you'll stop the night?'

'I'd like to. I'm not in court tomorrow and I can rearrange the two appointments I have in the office.'

'What a godsend you are! I confess that I wasn't much looking forward to my return to Deepwood this evening.'

When they parted after lunch it was agreed that Margaret should come along to Rosa's office at five o'clock.

'I know my partner would like to meet you', Rosa said as she hailed a taxi for her godmother.

In the event, however, Robin didn't return to the office that afternoon and Rosa left him a note saying what had happened and where she could be contacted during the next twenty-four hours. She also left her Deepwood telephone number with Stephanie, their Girl Friday without whom the smooth running of the office quickly faltered.

It was near enough seven thirty when they reached Deepwood Grange. There were two police cars parked outside the house and two other cars nearby which were clearly there on official business. Rosa decided to leave her car on the opposite side of the front door. As she and

Margaret approached the portico, a uniformed constable stepped from the shadows.

'Excuse me, madam, may I ask who you are?' he said in a polite but firm voice.

'I'm Mrs Lakington and I live here,' Margaret replied in a matching tone, adding, 'and this is my solicitor, Miss Epton.'

The officer shot Rosa an interested glance before turning back to Margaret and saying, 'If Detective Chief Inspector James wishes to interview you, will he find you in your apartment?'

'Yes.'

He stood aside and they went in. The Great Hall was deserted save for Tim Moxon who was hovering uncertainly outside the door of Apartment B in which David Anderson's body had been found.

'Good evening, Tim, I'm back and I've brought Rosa with me', Margaret called out. 'You remember meeting her at the party?'

'Yes, of course', he said, giving Rosa a wan smile.

Rosa felt that her godmother's forthrightness need not have stretched quite as far as informing the officer outside that she, Rosa, was her solicitor, nor as implying to Tim Moxon that she had a motive in bringing her god-daughter back with her. Both statements were open to misconstruction in the present situation.

'So what's the latest news?' Margaret now enquired.

'The police and various scientific experts are still going over the apartment. They've been there all day. It's just too horrible!'

'Have they found out exactly how David died?'

'The theory is that he must have been knocked out first and the plastic bag put over his head while he was unconscious. He died of suffocation. At least, that's what one of the detectives told me.'

'Does anyone know how David got into the apartment? I thought it was supposed to be locked.'

'It was locked', Moxon said in a voice that was almost a squeal.

'Then how did he get in?'

'It's no good asking me, Mrs Lakington. That's something the police will have to find out. I'm sorry, I didn't mean to be rude.'

'That's all right, you must have had an exhausting day. How fortunate that you were here on the spot when the body was discovered!'

It was not a sentiment with which Tim Moxon showed any inclination to agree.

'I phoned Mr Goran in Geneva immediately,' he said, 'and he's asked to be kept in touch with every development.'

'Is he coming over?'

'He'll decide when I phone him later this evening.'

Margaret glanced about her at the rows of firmly closed front doors.

'Why don't you come and join Rosa and me for a drink?' she said. 'I'm sure we could all do with one.'

'It's very kind of you, Mrs Lakington, but I couldn't possibly. I must stay here in case the police want me.'

Suddenly the neighbouring door opened and Alison Tremlett appeared.

'I thought I heard your voice, Margaret. Oh, and there's your nice god-daughter, Rosemary, too.'

'Her name's Rosa and we're both exhausted after driving down from town.'

'Come and have a drink and I'll tell you everything that's happened.'

'Has anyone been arrested yet?' Margaret enquired, as she half-turned away.

'No. The police have been interviewing people all day and I'm sure they'll want to talk to you once they know you're back.' It was as though she sought to reassure Margaret that she wouldn't be left out of any distribution of police favours. 'It's all so macabre', she went on in a tone of relish. 'They're trying to establish when he must have died. They've questioned me several times, seeing that I live in the next apartment to where the body was found. They think I must have heard something. Anyway, what sort of sound is made when you put a body up a chimney?'

'I imagine they'd be interested in any sounds at all coming from an empty apartment.'

'I know, and I've tried so hard to think back.' Ms Tremlett gave the impression of going into a light trance. 'I think I did hear muffled noises coming from there once, but I can't remember which night it was.'

'It could even have been your imagination at work', Margaret remarked unkindly.

'Poor David! He would never have been the victim in any story of mine.'

'Come on, Rosa, it's time we went up to my apartment', Margaret said firmly. Halfway up the staircase to the gallery, she observed, 'I trust the police realise what an unreliable witness she'd make. Unreliable *and* dangerous.'

'The police aren't easily taken in', Rosa remarked. 'For the most part they're as sceptical as lawyers.'

It was about half an hour later that the front door bell rang.

'I'll go', Rosa said, getting up from her chair.

'Mrs Lakington?' enquired a man with short, fair hair, blue eyes and a firm jawline. He had the air of someone who would have no trouble keeping order in a class of unruly children.

'No, but she's expecting you if you're Detective Chief Inspector James.'

His eyes widened slowly, then he smiled. 'May I come in then?'

'I'm Rosa Epton. I'm Mrs Lakington's god-daughter.'

'Epton? Epton? I seem to know that name. Weren't you concerned in a motoring case at Worthing a few years ago? A motoring case with unusual complications?'

'Yes.'

'I was at headquarters in our Special Branch section at the time.'

'So you remember the name Peter Atkins?'

'Yes, and his other name.'

'Who is it, Rosa?' Margaret called out from the living room.

'Detective Chief Inspector James.'

'Then stop exchanging reminiscences in the hall and bring him in!'

'Good evening, Mrs Lakington', James said, following Rosa into the room.

'Where would you like to sit, Chief Inspector?' Margaret asked, giving him an appraising look.

He pulled up a hardback chair and sat down. 'I can't interview people sunk into a sofa', he said with a faint smile.

'Would you like a drink or would that be in breach of regulations?'

'I won't have anything at the moment, thank you. I'm hoping to get home shortly for a meal. I called my wife just before I came up from the flat below.' He fixed Margaret with an alert look. 'I gather you've been in London all day?'

'Yes, I had an eleven o'clock appointment with my dentist and then I met Miss Epton for lunch. After that I went to the Tate Gallery for an hour or so before joining Miss Epton at her office. She very kindly drove me home. I hope that's a satisfactory account of my movements?'

'Entirely', he said with a faintly amused expression. 'I understand the body had been discovered before you left?'

'Yes, but I saw no need to cancel my day's arrangements as there was nothing I could contribute by remaining here. Also, I told Mr Dixon and Mr Murray where I was going. I hope you don't think I was running away for any reason?'

'Of course not', Chief Inspector James said with a deprecating gesture. 'How well did you know the dead man, Mrs Lakington?'

'I don't think anyone here knew him very well. He kept himself to himself and made it clear that he didn't wish to become too involved in such corporate life as we have. He was always perfectly polite, but he seemed to be a loner.'

'Miss Tremlett has described him as a man of mystery. Would you agree?'

'I think it was a description I used to Miss Epton', Margaret said, unwilling to let Alison Tremlett receive any credit for originality.

'When did you last see Mr Anderson?'

'It was one afternoon not long before we realised he was missing from his apartment. We happened to meet in the Great Hall and exchanged a hello. I was coming in and he was just locking his front door to go out.'

'His own apartment being on the opposite side of the Great Hall from the one in which his body was found?'

'Yes.'

'And how did he seem?'

'His normal self.'

'Not worried or anxious or anything of that sort?'

'Not in the slightest.'

'Hmm! As far as I've been able to find out the last time he was seen alive was around five o'clock on Friday, the second of November. Saturday's milk and newspaper stayed on his doorstep, as did Monday's and Tuesday's, at which point Miss Tremlett phoned Mr Moxon who came down.'

'Does the medical evidence indicate that he'd been dead for about twelve days?' Rosa asked with interest.

'Certainly that he could have been. You know pathologists, Miss Epton, they largely depend on what they're told in order to establish a time of death. Told by

40

the police that someone was seen alive at ten and found with a knife through his heart at two and they tell you he's been dead between one and four hours.' He paused. 'The interesting thing in this case is the sealing of the fireplace. A week ago today, on Monday, the fifth of November, workmen came and sealed it with a metal sheet. They were supposed to have done it before but had been held up for some reason or another. They'd hardly finished the job, it seems, when the couple who've bought the flat changed their minds about the form of heating they wanted and so this morning along came another lot of workmen to unseal it and see if the chimney provided suitable ventilation for one of those new-fangled gas fires. I don't know if you've seen it, but it's an enormous fireplace; I gather the room was the original drawing room when it was all one house. Anyway one of the men shoved his head and shoulders up the chimney to examine it. He shone his torch on what he first thought was a bundle of clothing and then realised it was a dead body.'

'The poor man must have been shattered', Margaret said.

'He was. He withdrew so rapidly that he gashed his head and had to go to hospital.'

'Was there any sign of decomposition?' Rosa enquired with professional interest.

'Virtually none. The air circulation in the chimney could have led to him becoming almost mummified, particularly in this sort of weather.'

'Tim Moxon said that he'd probably been rendered unconscious before having the plastic bag tied over his head', Rosa went on with the keenness of a terrier following an interesting scent.

'That's one theory we're working on, but we shan't know for certain until the pathologist has completed various tests. There were no signs of injury on the body and nothing to suggest he'd put up a struggle, so the

41

inference is that he was unconscious when he was trussed up and the bag put over his head. He could have been given a squirt of some knock-out gas. The sort used by dentists and criminals these days', he added with a wry smile. 'So what would be your theory, Miss Epton?'

'That whoever killed him and put the body up the chimney did so because he knew it was about to be sealed. It was a ready prepared tomb.'

'Like in that Verdi opera', Margaret broke in. 'The one where Aida and Radames sing a final duet as their tomb is sealed.'

'Operas always end in death, I'm told', Chief Inspector James remarked drily.

'Double deaths as often as not', Margaret said.

Rosa, who had been looking thoughtful, now broke in, 'Alternatively the body was put up the chimney as a temporary hiding place, but before it could be moved the men had come and sealed the fireplace. In which event the murderer must have received a nasty shock.'

'What I'd want to know if I were the police,' Margaret said energetically, 'is how did David Anderson get into the apartment and what was he doing there?'

'If we knew what he was doing there,' James said wearily, 'we'd almost certainly know why he was killed; even who killed him.'

'Did he have a key in his possession?' Rosa asked.

'He had no key on him that would open the door of Apartment B. And there was no sign of a forcible entry.'

'He must have had an accomplice', Margaret said firmly.

'I assure you, Mrs Lakington, that we're not overlooking any possibility', James replied. 'This was a brutal murder and I'm determined to nail the person who did it.' He paused. 'Can you think of anyone who had a grudge against Mr Anderson; anyone who might have had a reason for wanting to kill him?'

'Absolutely not. Surely what you need to find out is

why he was living here. It's not the sort of place for a lone man of his age. How old was he, incidentally?'

'Twenty-nine.'

'There you are! Not even thirty. What was he doing burying himself in the country in a place like Deepwood Grange which is full of ancients like me?'

'I think you exaggerate, Mrs Lakington. Mr Dixon and Mr Murray are scarcely ancient, nor is Miss Tremlett, nor the Unterbys.'

'You know quite well what I mean', she said severely. 'The fact was that David Anderson stuck out like a sore thumb amongst the rest of us. I'd have thought you needed to probe his background.'

Chief Inspector James got up. He felt that there was nothing further to be gained by staying. Moreover, he was remarkably hungry.

The fact was that he had already put in train as many enquiries as he hoped might prove fruitful. David Anderson's background was high on the list, though his apartment had revealed no clues whatsoever. It was as though he had had no previous existence before arriving there.

James had also given instructions that every laundry and garment cleaner within twenty-five miles should be visited with a view to finding out whether anyone had delivered clothing within the past ten days that bore signs of soot or chimney mortar. The officers engaged on the enquiry had been supplied with a list of all the residents at Deepwood Grange. Meanwhile, the grounds had been searched for signs of recently dug earth and the debris and ashes of two bonfires had been taken away for scientific examination.

From his questioning of Margaret Lakington and his cross-questioning of other residents, he had no cause to regard her as a suspect. Indeed, until he had found out a great deal more about the dead man, suspects would remain as spectral as autumn leaves in a desert. He

43

wasn't even prepared to exclude the possibility that the murderer came from without the closed community of residents, though somehow he thought not.

David Anderson's was not the only background he intended to probe.

CHAPTER 4

It wasn't long after Chief Inspector James had departed that the telephone rang.

'You answer it, Rosa dear', Margaret said. 'I'm not in the mood to talk to any of my neighbours.'

'It mayn't be a neighbour', Rosa said, getting up from her chair.

'It's sure to be. Probably Alison wanting to know what the police said to me. I shall feel inclined to tell her to flee while the going's good.'

Rosa went out into the hall and lifted the receiver.

'Margaret?' said a familiar voice.

'No, it's Rosa Epton, Sir Wesley.'

'As a matter of fact it's you I wanted to have a word with, Miss Epton. I heard that you had driven Margaret back from London and I wondered if you could spare me half an hour of your time.'

'This evening, do you mean?'

'As soon as is convenient. I have a rather delicate matter I wish to put to you.' After a pause he added, 'It's become considerably more urgent as a result of what has happened. If you could come now, we could talk without being interrupted. My wife's busy in the kitchen making cakes for a charity fair and I'll tell her we don't want to be disturbed.'

'All right, I'll come along in a few minutes', Rosa said,

44

none too enthusiastically.

She went back into the living room and told her godmother.

'I wonder what he's after', Margaret mused. 'Poor Sally, banished to the kitchen.'

'I gathered she was already there', Rosa remarked.

'Well, all you have to do is bang on the dividing wall if you need help.'

'It seems unlikely he'll get up to anything mischievous with his wife making cakes within earshot.'

'I wouldn't put anything past him. Don't forget I've had three husbands! You'd better take my key in case I'm in bed when you get back. It's been an exhausting day and I shan't stay up late.' She took one of Rosa's hands and gave it an affectionate squeeze.

A couple of minutes later Rosa was ringing the Binfields' door-bell. The door opened almost immediately to reveal Sir Wesley in a plum-coloured velvet jacket with matching slippers.

'Come in, Miss Epton. It's good of you to come so promptly.'

From the kitchen came the sound of the waltz theme from *Der Rosenkavalier* and with it a delicious smell of baking.

'My wife seems to believe that music assists her cooking,' he observed sardonically, 'but we shan't hear it in the drawing room. Have that chair, Miss Epton.' He indicated a small, uncomfortable-looking armchair. 'And what will you drink? What about a glass of Madeira?'

Rosa hadn't tasted Madeira since she first arrived in London and used to visit an ancient relative of her mother's who consumed it at all hours. She always supposed that he eventually died of Madeira poisoning.

'As you're aware, Miss Epton,' Sir Wesley said, sitting down opposite her, 'a brutal murder has been committed and the odds are that the murderer is in our midst. I am in possession of certain information that my civic duty requires me to pass to the police. At the same time, however, I hesitate to do so directly. Moreover, it might be more circumspect if certain enquiries were made before I take any action. Enquiries of a delicate nature with which I'd prefer my name not to be directly associated.'

'Is this the matter you mentioned earlier to my godmother?'

'Yes, I merely told her that I might ask you to undertake an assignment on my behalf.' He paused. 'Tell me, do you have good contacts at Scotland Yard?'

'I know quite a number of officers, if that's what you mean. I'm not too popular with some of them, though.'

'You wouldn't be if you do your job properly. The police have never liked seeing people get off. Usually for the excellent reason that they know they're guilty.'

'Or think they know', Rosa interjected. Sir Wesley permitted himself a small, wintry smile.

'What I meant was, do you have any contacts at the Yard who will pass you information off the record?'

'What sort of information do you have in mind?' Rosa asked warily.

'Whether or not somebody has a criminal record?'

'I thought it might be that.'

'That doesn't answer my question, Miss Epton.'

'Sometimes I can find something out, but it's not always easy. Any officer found leaking such information to someone not entitled to it can get into nasty trouble.'

'I could probably find out through my own sources – I used to know all the top people at the Yard – but I'm anxious that my name shouldn't be associated with the enquiry.' He met Rosa's doubtful gaze. 'As a result of the murder, the matter has become an imperative.'

'Who's the person about whom you want this information?' Rosa asked in a tone that bestowed a fragile aura

46

on each word.

Sir Wesley was silent for a while as he slowly revolved the stem of his glass.

'Our move to Deepwood Grange had already become an embarrassment to me before the murder took place', he said at last. 'More than ever now I wish we'd never set foot in the place.' He paused. 'Imagine my dismay, Miss Epton, when I recognised a fellow resident as somebody I'd once defended on a murder charge. I refer to Potter. He and his wife moved here after us and I thought his face was familiar the first time I met him, even though a great many years had passed. About fifty to be exact. I was junior defending counsel in a case in which Potter was charged with the murder of another man. Though he got off, I never had any doubt about his guilt. If he *had* been convicted, there's little doubt he would have been hanged.'

'And he's never recognised you?' Rosa said.

'No. I was just a young counsel in a wig and gown. My leader carried the burden of the defence.'

'But wouldn't he recall your name?'

'I doubt whether he ever bothered to know it. He was a young East End thug who left the court after his acquittal without ever pausing to thank any of those who'd been concerned in his defence.' Sir Wesley was thoughtful for a moment before continuing. 'I was pretty pleased with the result at the time as any young counsel would be, but now I feel it might have been better if we hadn't saved him from the gallows.'

'What were the circumstances of the case?'

'He was alleged to have strangled another man and thrown his body down an excavation where it was subsequently found. The prosecution's case was that Potter had been borrowing money from the man – his name was Frederick Flower – and killed him when Flower began pressing for repayment. The defence was

47

that Flower made a homosexual pass at Potter, who resisted it strenuously with the result that he found himself with a body on his hands. Literally. In the witness box Potter said he had only put his hands lightly round the other man's neck to resist his advances when he suddenly collapsed. Thereafter he, Potter, panicked.' He gave Rosa a wry glance. 'I'm sure it's not a story with which you're unfamiliar, Miss Epton. Anyway, Douglas Potter thereafter passed out of my life and stayed out of it until now, when he turns up at Deepwood Grange with, I'm led to believe, a millionaire's bank account. How he made his money, I've yet to be told', he added in a significant tone. 'Obviously the officer investigating the murder should be made aware of Potter's past and it's a question of how such information should be imparted to him. But before doing anything about that, I should like to find out whether he's been engaged in further criminal enterprises, hence my interest in your contacts with the Criminal Record Office.'

'They won't have details of his acquittal for murder', Rosa said in a stalling sort of voice.

'I realise that, but what's he been up to since?'

'You believe his money has come from crime?'

'It wouldn't surprise me to learn that. I'm afraid I don't associate Douglas Potter with honest toil and solid citizenship.'

'You could be utterly wrong. After all, the other murder took place fifty years ago. And anyway, what motive could he have had for killing David Anderson?'

'What motive did anyone have for murdering him?' Sir Wesley said in a faintly hectoring tone. 'The point is, will you undertake my assignment? I would, of course, remunerate you for your time.'

'Won't Chief Inspector James, as a matter of routine, check all the residents with CRO?'

'I wouldn't expect him to do so in the first instance, if

48

at all. It surely depends on which direction his enquiries take him.'

Rosa took a deep breath. 'I'll see if I can find out anything, but I don't promise results.'

'I realise that', he said with a satisfied nod. 'You see, Miss Epton, the man I helped to defend fifty years ago was a born murderer. And you know what they say about leopards never changing their spots.'

A few minutes later he escorted Rosa to the door. 'I think it would be inadvisable to tell Margaret what we have discussed. I'm sure you'll be able to satisfy any curiosity on her part some other way.'

Rosa was hardly out of the front door before she was regretting her involvement in Sir Wesley's machinations. Why on earth couldn't he tell Chief Inspector James what he knew about Douglas Potter? After all, the police were used to treating their sources of information in the strictest confidence.

She let herself into the apartment and found to her relief that Margaret had already gone to bed. That gave her till morning to think what she was going to tell her. The more she thought about it, the more she felt Sir Wesley had really put her on the spot, and she didn't thank him for it.

CHAPTER 5

Rosa emerged from her room shortly after eight the next morning to find Margaret on the telephone. She went into the living room and was standing gazing out of the window when her godmother joined her.

'That was Alison', Margaret said with a touch of

49

asperity. 'Who else at this hour of the day! She's now convinced that the police suspect her in connection with the murder. It's amazing what that woman will do to draw attention to herself.'

'What's given her that idea?' Rosa enquired.

'Simply that David Anderson's body was found in the apartment which adjoins hers. Have you ever heard anything so ridiculous? I pointed out that John and Desmond lived on the other side and could equally well regard themselves as suspects. Anyway, how was your visit to Sir Wesley?'

'Oh he just wanted to find out whether we'd learnt anything from the police that he didn't know', Rosa replied airily.

Margaret frowned before saying in a dismissive tone, 'In some ways he's as bad as Alison. Let's go into the kitchen and I'll make some coffee. I feel we're going to need all the sustenance we can get today.'

It was another golden autumn morning and an hour later Margaret, who appeared to be in a restless mood, suggested that they went for a stroll outside.

'I feel suddenly claustrophobic', she said. 'I'm not going to sit around here all day just in case the police want to talk to me. I'd go mad. Quite frankly I'd like to get right away until everything's over, but I suppose that's out of the question.'

'It might look a little suspicious unless you could persuade them it was a long-standing arrangement.'

Margaret nodded in an abstracted way. 'It's a sobering thought that poor David Anderson was entombed in that chimney for about ten days without any of us knowing. Any of us save for the person who murdered him, that is.' She walked toward the door. 'I'll just go and put on a hat.'

Rosa had noticed that she always wore a hat outside. Perhaps her wig made her feel vulnerable.

As they came out on to the gallery, Mr and Mrs Potter emerged from their apartment on the farther side. Thelma Potter gave them a friendly wave.

''Morning, Mrs Lakington', Doug Potter called out as they approached one another. 'Hope you didn't have any nightmares.' Giving Rosa a roguish look, he went on, 'Expect we'll all have our lawyers here before long.' He fell into step beside her as they started down the staircase. 'Did you meet David Anderson when you were here last time, Miss Epton?'

'Yes, at the party.'

'Nice boy, but somebody obviously had it in for him.'

'Do you have any theories?' Rosa asked.

'I know it wasn't me or Thelma, if that's what you're asking. Find the motive and you'll find the murderer, that's what I said to the police.'

'I gather nobody quite knows what he was doing here.'

'Somebody knew all right', he said grimly. 'Thelma and I came here for a bit of peace and quiet. I've had enough excitement in my life to last me. Certainly didn't want to walk into a murder.'

'What was your line of business?' Rosa asked.

'Making money, Miss Epton', he said, giving her a broad wink. 'I decided on that as a young man and set about doing it. You can't get anywhere worthwhile in life without money and that's a fact.' After a pause he went on, 'Hard work and luck is what you need. Stray over the line at the wrong moment and you end up in prison, but if your luck holds you finish up a millionaire. I'm one of the lucky ones. I'm seventy-six, got good health, a couple of nice homes and a Rolls Royce.'

'Where's your other home?' Rosa asked, encouraged by so much frankness.

'In Spain, but we're probably going to sell it. The area's attracting too much riff-raff. Thelma'd like a place in the West Indies. We'll fly out there after Christmas

51

and have a dekko. I'm prepared to spend up to three quarters of a million to get somewhere decent.' He rubbed his chin. 'Mind you, we'll still keep our apartment here. We like Deepwood Grange and I've spent a packet on the place. You should just see the kitchen. It's got every gadget that's ever been invented. How long are you staying?'

'I'm going back this afternoon.'

'Next time you're down, drop in and have a look at what we've done.'

'Do you think the murder might affect the value of the apartments?'

Doug Potter pursed his lips. 'Haven't really given that too much thought. It wouldn't put me off, but then I'm not everyone. I grew up in a tough area. It'd take more than a murder to deflect me if I wanted something badly enough. Thelma's a tough girl, too. You'd never think she was nearly seventy, would you?'

'Never', Rosa said, surveying the bobbing, golden curls ahead of her.

'Enjoy your job, do you?' Doug Potter asked suddenly.

'Very much. I like the human side. One meets all manner of people in a criminal practice.'

'Can't say I ever paid much attention to the ones who had to defend me.' The remark was accompanied by one of his broad winks. 'I might have done if any of 'em had been a pretty girl like you.' He sighed. 'But that was all a long, long time ago. I was constantly in and out of trouble as a youngster. Petty theft and fighting mostly.' He cast Rosa an amused glance. 'You surprised at me telling you all this?'

'I suppose I am, in a way.'

'It's because I've never been ashamed of what I've done. Nobody could ever call me a hypocrite. Not like that old judge of ours, Sir Wesley Binfield. You have to be a hypocrite, of course, to be a judge. All that preaching to the convicted before sending them down for a stretch. Telling 'em how wicked they've been when the odds are the judge himself is just as bad. His sins don't happen to have caught up with him, that's the only difference.'

They reached the bottom of the staircase and walked over to the centre of the Great Hall where Thelma and Margaret were deep in conversation. Doug Potter beamed at them for a while like a proud parent before breaking in.

'Come on, sweetheart', he said, giving his wife a pat on her behind. 'We want to try and find Tim Moxon before the police nab him.'

'Nab him?' Margaret said in a startled voice.

'Claim his attention for the rest of the morning. Did you think I meant arrest him?' he said with a hoarse chuckle.

'I'm sure Tim could never murder anyone,' Thelma remarked to no one in particular.

'If the motive's strong enough, anyone can commit murder', her husband said firmly. 'You agree with that, don't you, Miss Epton?'

Rosa gave a preoccupied nod, but said nothing. Her thoughts had drifted elsewhere and she felt suddenly oppressed by the atmosphere of surrealism that seemed to pervade Deepwood Grange. She followed Margaret outside and they strolled over to the wooden fence that separated a field of cows from the drive.

'I'd have expected the police to have swarmed back by now', Margaret said, as she leaned against a post and looked toward the house.

'They're probably pursuing their enquiries further afield', Rosa said. 'But you can be certain they will be back.'

At that moment John Dixon and Desmond Murray came out of the house and walked across to where the two women were standing.

'Hello, Rosa', Desmond said. 'We heard you were here. Alison told us she'd seen you.'

'No need for a public address system with that woman around', Margaret observed.

'We're going out for the day', John said. 'Felt we wanted to get right away.'

'Where are you going?'

'We haven't decided. We'll just drive until we stop.'

'I suspect that Alison must be the only person enjoying all the drama', Margaret said.

Desmond laughed. 'She told us that she'd decided to add a murder to the novel she's writing.'

'Is that the one about a thinly disguised Deepwood Grange?' Rosa asked.

'I think it must be, because she said she was making herself the murderer so that nobody could possibly complain.'

'Has she decided who she's going to kill?'

'If she has, she didn't tell us.'

Turning to Margaret, John said, 'Did you know that David Anderson never received any mail all the time he was here?'

'I certainly didn't. Who told you that?'

'It came out when we were talking to one of the police officers. In fact it's odder than that. He used to collect his letters from the main post office in Chichester, where they were addressed to him under a false name.'

'How very curious!' Margaret said. 'Did the police tell you that, too?'

'They didn't actually tell us', he said with a deprecating smile. 'We overheard an officer reporting it to the chief inspector when he was in our apartment yesterday evening.' He glanced at his watch. 'Come on, Des, we'd better be going or we'll be late.'

Late for what? Rosa wondered as she watched them

set off toward the garages.

Various cars arrived and the occupants disappeared inside the house. Rosa assumed they were police and forensic experts.

After lunch she said she felt she ought to get back to London. Margaret didn't demur and promised she would overcome her dislike of the telephone sufficiently to keep Rosa in touch with developments. In any event, it was agreed that Rosa should come down for the day on Sunday.

As she drove back to London that afternoon, Rosa hoped that she would find her partner in the office when she arrived. She had ever increasing doubts about undertaking Sir Wesley Binfield's assignment and wanted Robin's advice on what she ought to do. She hoped for the sake of everyone at Deepwood Grange that the murder wouldn't remain unsolved for long. Not everyone would share Doug Potter's robust sentiments. She didn't for one moment believe he had committed the crime, despite Sir Wesley's insinuations. But somebody had – and in a most ruthless manner.

CHAPTER 6

On the afternoon that Rosa drove back to London, Detective Chief Inspector James was sitting opposite a nervously sweating Tim Moxon in the Mayfair offices of Glass, Merrifield and Co.

By contrast with the person he was interviewing, CI David James was cool and composed. He was just thirty-five and had enjoyed rapid promotion since first joining the police. By the time he reached his early forties he hoped to be on a rung of the ladder which would enable him to apply for senior posts in other forces eventually ending up as a chief constable.

Though ambitious, he had always guarded his home life, the more so since his first wife had died of cancer three years earlier, leaving him with two sons, Paul and Jonathan, who were now respectively eleven and nine years old.

Looking back, he didn't really know how he had managed to cope during the two years after her death. Giving his sons the additional care and attention they needed and at the same time being a hard-worked detective inspector (he'd been promoted detective chief inspector six months previously) meant that something had to give. In his case it was sleep. He had disciplined himself to get by on five hours a night in order to be able to run his home with the minimum of outside help and also do his job.

But a year ago he had met Alice who was working backstage at the Chichester Festival Theatre. She was only twenty-two at the time, but three months after their first encounter they were quietly married and she was now expecting a baby. From the outset she had been accepted by Paul and Jonathan, who had come to regard her as a big sister. If they hadn't taken to her, David James doubted whether he would have asked her to marry him. And if he hadn't done that, he didn't know how much longer he could have continued living as he was. But it now seemed that providence had decided something must be done and he had never had any doubts that Penny, his first wife, would have approved.

He now had a supremely contented home life and a job which fulfilled all his other needs. And when something like the Deepwood Grange case came along his cup overflowed with professional satisfaction, for there weren't many murders in the area and certainly none with as many intriguing aspects as the one he was now investigating.

'Is it terribly hot in here?' Tim Moxon said, passing a hand across his glistening forehead.

'Just right for me', CI James said equably.

'It's the wretched air-conditioning. It's never right', Moxon went on with an unhappy smile.

'I work in an office where the only air-conditioning is the window', James replied. It wasn't true, but that didn't bother him. He wanted Tim Moxon to go on feeling ill-at-ease. The longer he did so, the greater his chance of finding out why. 'Now, tell me more about David Anderson.'

'There's nothing more to tell', Moxon replied with a squirm. 'He bought his apartment and moved in about two months ago.'

'There must have been much more to the transaction than that.'

'Honestly there wasn't. He just came into the office one day and said he'd read about Deepwood Grange in a magazine and were there any apartments still unsold? I told him that Apartment E on the ground floor was still going and the next day we drove down for him to see it. He immediately took it.'

'Stop there for a moment, Mr Moxon. What did you talk about on the way down in the car?'

'You can't expect me to remember that!'

'I'm sure he must have told you something about himself for example.'

'Not that I recall.'

'Recall a little harder, Mr Moxon. This is a murder enquiry and I'm certain you can help me if you want. If you choose not to, I shall draw my own conclusions.'

Tim Moxon wiped away the beads of perspiration that had appeared on his upper lip.

'He just took the apartment and paid the asking price

without question, so that I had no need to ask him any personal questions', he said in a pleading tone.

CI James gazed at him thoughtfully for a while.

'Do you value your job?'

'Yes, of course', Tim Moxon said with a gulp.

'Then start being frank with me or you won't have it much longer. I'm sure Mr Goran wouldn't want to be told that you'd been obstructing the police in their enquiries. Incidentally, are you expecting him over?'

'He hasn't said he's coming.'

'So back to my question. What did David Anderson tell you about himself?'

'I think he mentioned that he'd had a bit of a nervous breakdown and had been advised to go and take things easy in the country for a while.'

'Is that what he told you?'

'I seem to remember his saying that.'

'What job did he have before?'

'I think he said he worked in the City.'

'In what capacity?'

'As a clerk of some sort.'

'Clerks don't earn enough to buy a chicken coop at Deepwood Grange, let alone one of its apartments. How much did he pay for his?'

'Eighty five thousand pounds. I always assumed he had private means.'

'Unless, of course, somebody bought it for him.'

'That's something I wouldn't know', Tim said with a helpless shrug, casting a glance about the room as though in hope of quick relief.

'I take it you have a file, letters and the like, relating to his purchase of the apartment?'

'Er, yes . . . somewhere.'

'I'd like to see it.'

Moxon went across to a steel filing cabinet which stood in a corner of his room and pulled out the top drawer. He extracted a thin, buff folder and returned to his desk.

'There are no secrets in this', he said with a strained smile.

'Then you won't object to my looking at it', CI James replied, holding out his hand for it. He glanced quickly through its meagre contents. 'Did all the purchases go through with as little paperwork?' he asked.

'Far from it. But as I've mentioned, David Anderson made up his mind as soon as he saw the apartment. He just signed the agreement, paid and moved in.'

The thing that had struck James when he had searched the deceased's apartment the previous day had been the absence of personal data. It was almost as if it had been lived in by somebody who had been at pains to conceal his identity. Either that, or his killer had taken time to remove all such items. He could certainly have done so in the ten days before the body was found. It was only by chance that James had found a crumpled envelope beneath the driving seat of Anderson's car which was addressed to John Appleton, c/o the Post Office, Chichester. It had led the police to discover that this was the name by which he received mail. But it didn't answer the question as to why he hadn't wished letters to be sent to him at Deepwood Grange, unless he was afraid of their falling into the wrong hands.

James observed from the file that his bank was the Notting Hill Gate branch of the Southern Counties Bank and that his address at the time was shown as Flat 6, 16 Osming Street, W2. This was the same address shown on his driving licence, which had been the only document in his wallet to reveal any personal details.

He was preparing to visit the bank after leaving Glass, Merrifield and Co in the hope of gleaning further information about the dead man. At the moment he didn't even know his next of kin. Presumably somewhere there was a will he had made. A local firm of solicitors had handled the conveyance of the apartment and James had already ascertained that they knew nothing more about it than that he had walked into their office one day and asked them to deal with the matter on his behalf. They had done so, been paid and that was that.

CI James became aware of Tim Moxon's nervous gaze as he leafed through the file he had in his hand and which told him virtually nothing he didn't already know. It merely confirmed that David Anderson's purchase of an apartment at Deepwood Grange had been carried through without any of the usual hiccoughs associated with such a transaction. A few minutes later he got up and made to leave.

'Don't think you've seen the last of me, Mr Moxon', he said as he reached the door.

'You know where you can reach me', Moxon said in a resigned tone. 'I'll probably be down at the house tomorrow if you want me. I'm afraid all this has rather unsettled the residents and if I'm not around, they'll be endlessly on the phone to the office.' He let out a deep sigh. 'And, of course, I also have to keep Mr Goran in touch with what's happening.'

If he hoped for a sympathetic response from CI James, he was knocking on the wrong door. All he got was a glance of steely appraisal.

The manager of the Notting Hill Gate branch of the Southern Counties Bank was a short, tubby man with a shining bald head and a pair of gold-rimmed spectacles.

He glanced at the warrant card CI James showed him and sat back in his chair with the air of someone who spent their time dealing with detective chief inspectors.

'You realise, of course, that I can't disclose any of Mr Anderson's affairs with the bank without the appropriate court order and I take it you haven't yet procured one', he said briskly.

'I hope you'll be able to answer my questions, Mr Saunders, without breaking any confidences', James said in a disarming tone. 'I'm not after details of Mr Anderson's account at this stage, merely pursuing various peripheral enquiries over which I feel you may be able to help me. First, let me ask this: does the bank hold his will? I'm not asking about its contents, only its whereabouts.'

A portentous frown gathered on Mr Saunders's brow as he pondered the question.

'No, we don't hold it', he said at last. CI James had the impression that he somehow regarded the admission as a sign of failure.

'Do you know who are his next of kin?'

'I would assume his parents. They live in Hong Kong.'

'Does he have any family in this country?'

'I don't think so. He once told me that he was an only child and that his parents had sent him to this country to be educated and that, apart from holidays, he had never gone back to Hong Kong.'

'Do you know if his father was a wealthy man?'

'From what he said on various occasions, I would think he was extremely well off.'

'What exactly did David Anderson do for a living?'

Mr Saunders's frown returned.

'He was a clerk in the City to the best of my knowledge.'

'Were his finances in keeping with a clerk's?' James asked, half-expecting a rebuff.

The frown, however, disappeared and was replaced by a small, superior smile.

'There are clerks and clerks, Chief Inspector', Mr Saunders replied.

'Do you know which brand he was?'

The frown immediately returned and there was a

pause before he answered.

'Quite frankly, he was a bit of a man of mystery. He was always charming whenever I met him, but he never talked much about what he did. What I'm telling you is entirely a personal impression based on our infrequent meetings.'

'What would prompt such meetings?' James enquired, hoping that the manager wouldn't shy away from such a bold question.

Mr Saunders pulled a face as if he had bitten into a lemon, then gave a shrug.

'I suppose there's no harm in my telling you that, in the circumstances. He used to come and see me when he wanted to borrow money. That's the reason most of my customers want to see me', he added drily. 'From time to time, we lent Mr Anderson large sums of money. They were always short-term loans and were repaid by the due date.'

'Do you have any idea for what purpose he wanted the money?'

'I only know what he told me.'

'Which was?'

'What I'm about to tell you is strictly off the record and not for any official use. Is that clearly understood?' James nodded and the manager went on, 'I understood he required the money to do with his job.'

'We seem to be going round in a circle. What job?'

'I don't know any more than I've told you.'

'I assume you held collateral for these loans?'

'Of course. We held the deeds to his flat in Osming Street, which was more than sufficient to cover what we lent him.'

On leaving the bank, CI James enquired the way to Osming Street and was relieved to find that it was within easy walking distance.

It turned out to be quite a short street with small but

expensive houses on either side. At the farther end was a squat block of flats which he guessed had probably been erected on a wartime bomb site. The figures 16 were painted in gold above the glass-door entrance. Set into a pillar on the right were six bellpushes with a slot beside each for the occupant's name. There were no names, however, beside the bells for flats 5 and 6.

A man with a mop and bucket was swabbing the back of the entrance hall and CI James knocked on the door to attract his attention. The man glanced round, then came to the door and opened it.

'Yes?' he said in a not particularly friendly tone.

James produced his warrant card.

'Police? Who is it you want to see?'

'Were you aware that Mr Anderson of Flat 6 was dead?'

'No. Nobody's told me. He was only a young chap. What did he die of?'

'Suffocation.'

The man gave James a suspicious look. 'How'd he suffocate?'

'Someone tied a plastic bag over his head.'

'That'd be murder.'

'It was.'

'Cor! Well, you needn't look at me. I've never murdered anyone.'

'I'm glad to hear it. When did you last see him?'

'About a couple of weeks ago. He used to call in to collect things.'

'Who removed his name from the slot beside his bell?'

'He did. When he moved away.'

'Is his flat up for sale?'

'No. He said he'd be coming back in a few months' time.'

'That's interesting. Tell me, had he been ill before he left?'

63

'No', the man said in a puzzled tone. 'He always kept himself real fit. Used to play squash and go running in the park. Never known him ill all the while I've been here.'

'Did you know where he's been living?'

'Somewhere in Sussex', he said.

'He didn't give you his address?'

'No. Wasn't any need as he used to come back here for his letters and things.'

'Do you have a key to his flat?'

'No.'

'Do you know if he left one with anybody?'

Apart from his car keys and a door key to Apartment E, James had failed to discover any others. The inference was that the murderer had removed them, including one to the flat in Osming Street.

'He may have given a key to the gentleman in Flat 5', the man said.

'Who lives there?'

'Mr Moxon.'

CHAPTER 7

It took Chief Inspector James nearly half an hour to find a public telephone which was neither occupied nor vandalised. He dialled Glass, Merrifield's number and asked to speak to Mr Moxon.

'I'm afraid he's out and won't be back this afternoon', a female voice said. 'Can I take a message?'

'No, don't worry. I'll try and catch him at home. I take it he's still living at the same flat in Osming Street?'

'Yes, that's right.'

'Many thanks for your help', James said, and meant it.

He hadn't thought it likely that the Mr Moxon who lived in Flat 5 was other than Tim Moxon, but now he had confirmed it.

Turning his back on the swarthy youth who was scowling at him through the glass wall of the kiosk he dialled his home.

'It's David', he said when he heard his wife's voice. 'I'm in a public call box, but I thought I'd let you know that I shan't be home till later than I expected. Is everything all right?'

'Everything's fine', Alice said in her reassuring way. 'The boys have just got in and are about to have their tea. I know Jonathan would like to have a word with you. Hold on and I'll call him. . . .'

'Hello, Dad, I scored two goals this afternoon', a breathless Jonathan announced a few seconds later.

'Two? That's terrific. Well done.'

'We won easily.'

'What was the score?'

'Two nil.'

'And you got both goals?'

'Yes. One was a header, too, Dad.'

Jonathan sounded proud and a trifle smug, but his father had no intention of deflating him. After all, he felt a small surge of pride himself.

'How did Paul's team get on?' he asked.

'They lost. . . . Paul wants to say something, Dad.'

'We only lost because our goalkeeper got hurt in the first twenty minutes', said an obviously miffed Paul. 'The boy who took his place couldn't have stopped a snowball.'

'That was tough luck losing your goalkeeper. I hope he wasn't badly hurt.'

'He twisted his knee', Paul said with a trace of scorn.

'I'd better go, as I'm running out of coins.'

'Where are you, Dad?'

'In London.'

'Lucky you.'

'Let me have a quick word with Alice before I'm cut off. . . . OK, darling, I'll see you around nine. Take care of yourself till I get back.'

He emerged from the kiosk and crossed the road to a café on the opposite side, where he sat down and ordered a cup of coffee. He decided from a quick look around that he was the only customer whose origins didn't lie in the Middle East. Even the graffiti on the walls outside was written in some Islamic language. That particular area of W2 seemed to have been taken over.

It was a ten-minute walk back to Osming Street. He reached number 16 and pressed the bell of Flat 5. There was no answer, nor any guarantee, of course, that Tim Moxon would be returning home until much later – if at all that evening.

Watching and waiting were, however, very much part of a policeman's life and though CI James was not a patient man by nature, it was one of the disciplines he had acquired in the course of his career. There was a public house on a corner diagonally across from the flats and he went in and ordered a beer. It was still early for the steady evening drinkers and he had the place almost to himself. He carried his beer across to a seat near the window and sat down. With luck he would spot Tim Moxon as he approached the flats and be able to take him by surprise.

He had been in the pub about twenty minutes when the door of the saloon bar was pushed open and his quarry walked in and went straight up to the bar without a glance to left or right.

'A large Scotch, Gloria, and double quick', he said to the barmaid who had served James. 'I've had the helluva day and need a drink like never before.'

'What's happened then?' the girl asked with casual

66

interest as she put two measures of whisky into a glass.

'Everything's happened. You know that place down in Sussex I've told you about, Deepwood Grange? They've had a murder there. And, of course, it's yours truly who's been left to cope with the police and everything else.'

'Who's been murdered?' the girl asked with livelier interest.

Tim Moxon looked quickly about him as if to make sure he couldn't be overheard and for the first time noticed CI James sitting by the window. He gaped and put his drink down so violently that some of it spilled on to the counter.

James got up and approached him.

'Good evening, Mr Moxon. I was hoping to catch you, though I hadn't reckoned on it being in here. Perhaps we could go over to your flat and talk there.'

It was several seconds before Tim Moxon found his tongue and when he spoke it sounded as if his vocal cords had been coated in sand.

'I'm afraid I'm going out to dinner. I haven't really the time', he said.

'You'd better phone and say you'll be late', James replied in an uncompromising tone.

'Er . . . yes . . . if I must.'

He made to move when CI James said, 'Don't you want to finish your drink? I heard you tell the barmaid that you'd had the helluva day and it could be that it isn't over yet.'

It was in silence that they crossed the road and Tim Moxon produced a key to open the street door.

'I'm afraid there's no lift', he remarked, as if hoping this might deter James from coming any further.

'Good. They're unreliable contraptions. You and David Anderson had the second floor to yourselves, didn't you?'

'Yes. But we were never more than neighbours.'

'Oh, no?'

'Honestly, I didn't know him at all well. I'd never met him before I moved here a year ago and we hardly ever socialised. He was always a bit of a loner. You do believe me, don't you, Chief Inspector?'

They had reached the front door of Flat 5 and Tim Moxon led the way in.

'Come into the living room', he said. The room in question was comfortably furnished and expensively decorated. Observing James's expression of appraisal he went on quickly, 'I'm able to get a lot of things at a discount.'

CI James selected a black leather swivel chair and sat down.

'If you'd not realised it before, Mr Moxon, I'm sure you do now; the time has come to tell the truth. I don't want any more evasions or prevarication. Why did David Anderson want an apartment at Deepwood Grange?'

Tim Moxon gave an unhappy squirm before replying.

'He knew my firm managed the property and simply said he'd like to buy one of the apartments.'

'You'll have to do better than "simply said" if you're still hoping to keep your dinner date. Why did he want an apartment there? More important, what was his job?'

'I always understood that he was some sort of investigator. He never really talked about his work, but I gathered he was some sort of private eye.'

'On his own or for an outfit?'

'I think he was a freelance.'

'Did he have an office?'

'In the City, I think, but I don't know the address. He always gave the impression that his work was rather hush-hush.'

'What about my other question: why did he want an apartment at Deepwood Grange?'

'He said it was in connection with his work.'

'As an investigator?'

'I imagine so.'

'Who was he investigating there?'

'I've no idea and that's the truth', Tim said in a tone verging on desperation.

'You must have formed some idea.'

'I haven't and he never gave me any clue. Quite honestly I hated the whole business and wish now I'd never sold him the apartment.'

'Why did you?'

Tim Moxon turned a yellowy colour and began to sweat profusely.

'He wanted it badly and was willing to pay the price', he said with apparent difficulty.

CI James was staring at him thoughtfully when the cause of Tim Moxon's increasing discomfiture suddenly dawned on him. David Anderson had probably paid over the price and Moxon had made a personal profit out of the deal. The agent's venality, however, was not his preoccupation at that moment.

'There were other unoccupied apartments at the time, weren't there? What made Anderson choose the one he did?'

'He liked it the best.'

'It's directly beneath Mrs Lakington's, isn't it?'

'Yes.'

'And the one in which his body was found lies beneath the Binfields'?'

'Yes.'

'Did he view that one?'

'Yes, but it was bigger than he wanted and more expensive than the one he took.'

'Does the chimney in which his body was hidden connect with a Binfield chimney?'

'Yes. With the one that serves their living-room fire.'

CI James fixed Tim with a hard stare. 'How did Anderson get into Apartment B?' he asked.

'After I'd shown him round, he asked if I would leave him keys to all three unoccupied apartments, as although he was virtually certain he wanted Apartment E, he'd like to have another look around the next day before finally committing himself. You see, I had to return to London that evening and David said he'd stop the night at the local pub and come back the next day. As he was my neighbour in Osming Street I didn't think twice about letting him have the keys. I can only assume he had a duplicate made before returning them to me.' Tim paused and gave his inquisitor a look of misery. 'As soon as he got back to London he returned the keys to me and confirmed his offer for Apartment E.' He gave an anguished squirm. 'If I'd known what he'd done, I'd have been very angry. It was a complete breach of trust.'

James reflected that Tim Moxon's anger would probably not even have blown out a candle. It was a while before he spoke again.

'Do you have a key to the next door flat here?'

'No.'

'Quite sure?'

'I give you my word of honour.'

'The janitor to whom I spoke thought Anderson might have left one with you when he moved to Sussex.'

'He didn't. In fact, he's never left me a key when he's gone away.'

'I want to take a look around his flat.'

'You'd better speak to the managing agents.'

'Isn't that your firm?'

'No. It's Crane & Co in Kensington Church Street.'

'I'd have thought you'd be living in one of your own firm's properties', James said, with a puzzled expression.

Tim Moxon assumed a pained look. 'I'm afraid they're all well beyond my means.'

'How many properties do you manage for Mr Goran?'

'Deepwood Grange is the only one.'

CI James once more lapsed into thought. On the whole he was pleased with his afternoon's work. He had made a useful start in unearthing the deceased's background. One way or another, however, he must get into his flat. Meanwhile he would contact the local police station and arrange for the front door of Flat 6 to be sealed.

He didn't want anyone else getting there ahead of him – if that had not already happened.

CHAPTER 8

Robin was out when Rosa returned to her office around half past three that afternoon.

'He's gone to a conference with Mr Melfrey', Stephanie said, referring to a counsel whom they often briefed. 'He's going straight home from there, but said to tell you that he'll be in all the evening if you want to speak to him. I think he's rather hoping that you will.'

'Then I mustn't disappoint him', Rosa remarked. 'Anything startling happened during my short absence from the office?'

'Ben had a brush with the police yesterday evening', Stephanie observed drily. 'He parked his motor-cycle right in front of one of their cars from which they were maintaining observation on a house. They told him to move, but Ben didn't like their tone of voice and said so.'

'He wasn't arrested?' Rosa enquired a trifle anxiously.

'No. There was just an exchange of words', Stephanie said in her deadpan voice.

Ben had been a client of Rosa's, who, after serving a borstal sentence, had come to the office asking for a job. Rosa had persuaded Robin that they should take him on as office-boy and general outdoor messenger. He had now been with the firm nearly a year and a half to each side's satisfaction. He was twenty and had a steady girl-friend named Pauline who came a close second to his beloved motor-bike in his affections. The motor-cycle was a huge, gleaming monster, astride which Ben resembled a black-winged envoy from outer space.

'Is Ben in?' Rosa now asked.

'No, he's out on one of his rounds.'

'I'd better go and see what's sitting on my desk.'

'Mickey Rogers is coming in to see you tomorrow afternoon. He said you told him to make an appointment before his next court appearance.'

Rosa had temporarily forgotten about Mickey and the diamond ring he had been minding for a friend. A friend whose name he couldn't remember.

Having spent a couple of hours in her office, Rosa got back to her flat about seven. She had an immediate hot bath as was her wont and was wondering what to have for supper when her phone rang.

'It's Robin. I thought I'd call you. How were things at Deepwood Grange when you left? Have the police made an arrest yet?'

'No. I don't think they've even got a prime suspect. Have you time to talk?'

'Yes, that's why I didn't wait for you to call.'

'There's one matter on which I particularly want your advice, Robin', Rosa said. 'It concerns Sir Wesley Binfield.'

When Rosa finished speaking, Robin's reaction was immediate.

'Don't have anything to do with it, Rosa! If the old boy wants to find out about Mr Potter's suspected life of

72

crime, let him make his own enquiries. I'm sure he's still got enough contacts at the Yard.'

'He said as much, but—'

'—Then let him use them!' Robin broke in. 'It's one thing for you and me to try and tap the grapevine in our own cases, but Sir Wesley's not even a client.'

'Well he is in a way. He said he'd be willing to pay for my professional services.'

'Then tell him you're sorry but you can't help him after all. Say that all lines of communication are blocked, all your contacts have gone deaf and you can't find out a thing.' He paused before adding, 'Think how silly you'd look if it turned out you'd been helping David Anderson's murderer.'

'You don't seriously think Sir Wesley might have done it?' Rosa exclaimed.

'No, but my advice to you is still the same. Give it a day or two, then write him a letter saying you're sorry et cetera.'

'Thanks, Robin', Rosa said after a moment's silence. 'On reflection, I think you're probably right.'

'Now tell me the rest of the goings-on there', he said. When Rosa had finished her account of events, he murmured in a reflective tone, 'I suppose it was an inside job.'

'It looks that way.'

'Do you regard Tim Moxon as belonging in that category?'

'Yes.'

'I imagine we can exclude your godmother from any list of suspects?'

'Certainly.'

It had, nevertheless, struck Robin as a curious coincidence that the murder had occurred so soon after Margaret Lakington had renewed contact with Rosa and invited her for a weekend at Deepwood Grange. For the time being, however, he decided to keep this reflection to himself.

'So who does that leave?' he went on. 'Tim Moxon, the two gay young men, Alison Tremlett and Mr Potter. What about that other couple, the husband's a solicitor and local councillor?'

'The Unterbys. They were on holiday in Marrakesh at the relevant dates. You've not mentioned Sir Wesley.'

'I know', he said thoughtfully. 'One thinks of members of the judiciary as being the victims of murder rather than the perpetrators. But given a strong enough motive, I imagine Sir Wesley could commit murder as well as anyone else. At least, be a party to it, even if he didn't use his own hands for the deed. It's interesting his having defended Potter on a murder charge all those years ago. And I wonder how Potter has made his millions? But let the police dig around in that particular dunghill! I imagine they'll be digging even harder into David Anderson's shadowy background. He strikes me as being the odd one out in the whole set-up.' Rosa could hear someone talking in the background. 'Susan says when are you coming down for Sunday lunch?' Robin said. 'And the children want to see you, too.'

'You ask me and I'll come', Rosa said cheerfully.

'Right. We'll fix something up when I see you in the office tomorrow.'

'Mr Rogers has arrived', Stephanie announced in her most formal tone at three thirty the next afternoon.

'Show him in', Rosa said, and got up from her desk.

'Mr Rogers to see you, miss', Ben said flinging open her door a minute later, at the same time giving Rosa a broad wink behind her visitor's back.

'Come in, Mickey', Rosa said. 'I'm glad you made an appointment.'

'You didn't think I wouldn't, did you, Miss Epton?' he

enquired in a slightly hurt voice.

'No, of course not. It's just that I wasn't expecting to see you quite so soon. There are still eight days to go before your next appearance in court and I'm apt to think of you as somebody who leaves things till the last moment. I recall your reluctance to come and discuss the allegation of corruption you'd made against one of the officers in your last case.'

'Yes, I remember now', he said in a dawning tone. 'I decided to let bygones be bygones. You didn't mind, did you?'

In fact Rosa had minded and had felt distinctly cross, particularly when the officer in question clearly believed she had put Mickey up to making the allegation.

'Yes, I did', she replied, 'but let bygones be bygones, as you've just said, and let's concentrate instead on the little matter of Mrs Osman's diamond ring. Have you remembered the name of the friend who gave it to you to look after?'

Mickey's expression cleared as he beamed at her.

'John Baraski. I told you it was foreign-sounding.'

'Have you seen him since?'

'No. 'Im and 'is girl 'as disappeared. She was foreign.'

'I know. Portuguese, Sergeant Grierson said.'

'From one of those sort of countries', Mickey replied with airy insularity.

'You'd better tell me exactly what Baraski said when he handed you the ring.'

'I guess I 'ad', he said none too happily. 'John knew I knew about diamonds and 'e asked me if I could put a value on it for 'im. I'd only 'ad the thing twenty-four hours when the law barged in with a search warrant and that was that.'

'Sounds as if somebody framed you.'

'My own view exactly, Miss Epton, and I reckon I knows who it was. A bloke named Sam Slater whose brother-in-law went down in that conspiracy job you defended me on. Slater's also related to John Baraski. You know what, Miss Epton?' he went on in an aggrieved tone. 'They're all a lot of right villains.'

'I take it Slater blames you for the fact his brother-in-law is in prison?'

'Sort of', Mickey said in a brooding way. 'It all goes back to that job you defended me on.'

'Then we'd better do the same', Rosa remarked.

'Frank Pearce, that's Slater's brother-in-law, got five years, you remember. He seemed to feel that because he'd been clobbered, I should have been as well. He was always a surly type.' He glanced up and met Rosa's gaze. 'I don't know how much of this you knew, Miss Epton, but Frank and me were part of a diversionary plan. It was worked out when it seemed things might go wrong. The main haul was over three million pounds' worth of diamonds. That part went as smooth as a baby's dream. They were smuggled out and sold for cash in Hong Kong.' He gave Rosa a reflective smile. 'Diamonds are the thing, Miss Epton. Much easier to 'andle than gold or your art treasures.'

'I've always heard they're a girl's best friend', Rosa observed.

'They're better than that. Do you realise that a million pounds' worth of diamonds can be put into a parcel no bigger than an ordinary book? And if they're under two carat diamonds, they won't be recorded and so can't be identified. Did you know that, Miss Epton?' he asked, his eyes positively gleaming.

'No.'

'They're foolproof.'

'Unless you get caught.'

'Only Frank and me and that other bloke ever got caught. And we was only part of the diversionary tactic. Mind you, we was well paid for our trouble. Frank

Pearce ought to remember that instead of trying to even scores from prison. The people who carried out the main job were never caught and never will be. Three million pounds' worth of diamonds just vanished between Hatton Garden and the airport. The funny part is, Miss Epton, that they were a consignment for 'Ong Kong, which is where they ended up, anyway, but by a different route one might say.'

'Was it all masterminded by one person?'

Mickey nodded. 'The Mr Big figure the papers love to write about.'

'Do you know his identity?'

'No, and I don't want to. It's not 'ealthy to know too much. Two brothers named Shipton were in charge of the operation. They 'ijacked the car carrying the diamonds to the airport, knocked the driver out and got clean away. When the driver come round, there was a traffic warden writing out a ticket for 'im being parked on a double yellow line. I don't think 'e appreciated the joke.' His expression clouded. 'When the police got on to me and Frank and the other bloke, they knew we'd been up to something, but they didn't 'ave any evidence, so they framed us.' He paused. 'They're bad losers, the police are, Miss Epton.'

Mickey had now explained much that had earlier been shrouded in mystery. The case against him had been extremely thin and Rosa could only reflect that if the police had framed him, they hadn't made a very competent job of it. It was not a case that brought back any pleasurable memories to her, even though Mickey had left the court a free man.

'Sergeant Grierson obviously believes he's got you bang to rights in the present case. Unless John Baraski steps forward nobody's going to believe your story, you do realise that?' After a slight pause she added, 'A court won't necessarily believe you, even if Baraski does appear.'

'They've got to, Miss Epton. It's the truth.'

'It's as implausible as the man who says his wife's mink coat fell off the back of a truck.'

'Things do fall off the backs of trucks', Mickey said with a grin.

'I know. Cases of whisky, television sets and expensive video equipment', Rosa retorted.

'Don't be too 'ard on me! I really 'ave been trying to go straight since I met this girl. I worship 'er. I wouldn't let 'er down for all the world.'

'When's the baby due?'

'Next March.'

'A pity she wasn't there to instil a bit of sense into you when Baraski persuaded you to take the ring.'

'You're right', he said dejectedly. 'She's too good for me.'

'Stop feeling sorry for yourself and I'll start taking a proof of your evidence.'

Forty minutes later the proof was completed and she and Mickey were fortifying themselves with cups of tea served by Ben.

'You mentioned two brothers named Shipton who took part in the diamond robbery', Rosa remarked. 'Is it with one of them that your wife ran away?'

'No. She's living it up in Spain with another of the blokes who was on the job. A geezer called Adrian who 'as an accent to match. Sylvie could never resist someone who talked like a duke, even if 'e was a shit. I've no idea what 'appened to Gordon and Gary Shipton afterwards. We just all split up. They could be in Spain, too.'

Rosa reflected that if the newspapers were to be believed a large percentage of England's criminal fraternity had migrated to the Iberian peninsula. She herself regularly received a Christmas card from one of her clients who had gone there.

CHAPTER 9

Sir Wesley Binfield called an emergency meeting of the residents' association for the following evening and issued what amounted to a royal command to Tim Moxon to be present.

Because he was chairman of the association and because the Binfields' apartment was one of the larger ones, meetings were invariably held in their drawing room. Chairs were brought in from other rooms and were placed in a haphazard semicircle so that everyone was more or less facing Sir Wesley, who seated himself at a card table with Alison Tremlett next to him.

Alison had been elected honorary secretary on the strength of being a writer, it being assumed (wholly erroneously as it turned out) that anyone who could write books would also be capable of composing the minutes of their meetings. Too late it was discovered that she had a remarkable facility for recording every irrelevant observation while omitting to note any decisions that were reached. It was a habit that drove Sir Wesley to distraction and he had gone so far as to suggest that the appointment should not be for more than twelve months at a time. He had quickly dropped that suggestion, however, when Doug Potter had asked why the same thing shouldn't apply to the chairman.

At eight thirty the next evening everyone was crowded into the Binfields' drawing room. Even the Unterbys, who had returned from holiday only that afternoon, put in an appearance. They were able to look smugly relaxed in the knowledge that no finger of suspicion could possibly point in their direction.

At one time coffee was served by Lady Binfield, but the practice had ceased after Alison spilt a cup over the carpet. This had not only delayed the start of the meeting, but a reference thereto had found its way into the minutes, to Sir Wesley's exasperation.

'If you'll all sit down, we'll begin', he announced above the murmur of conversation. When satisfied that order reigned, he went on, 'I thought we should have a meeting to discuss various matters that have arisen from recent unfortunate events.'

'What unfortunate events are you on about?' Doug Potter asked loudly.

Sir Wesley frowned in a manner that would have intimidated a lesser mortal.

'I think it's obvious to everyone else that I was referring to Mr Anderson's murder.'

'You said events in the plural', Doug said unabashed.

Deciding to ignore this piece of near lese-majesty, Sir Wesley continued, 'I judged it important that Mr Moxon should attend our meeting as I'm sure a number of you will have questions you wish to ask him. All such questions should, of course, be put to him through the chair.' He glanced about him and was gratified to observe that most of his audience was listening attentively. 'First, however, may I assume that it will be your wish that a wreath should be sent to Mr Anderson's funeral on behalf of all his fellow residents at Deepwood Grange? Will those in favour of the proposal please signify?' There was a flutter of half-raised hands. 'Then I suggest we ask Miss Tremlett to make the necessary arrangements.'

'But I don't even know when the funeral is', Alison wailed, as though emerging from a disturbing dream.

'Can you help us, Mr Moxon?' Sir Wesley said turning to Tim, who was sitting on a kitchen chair as far from the chairman as he could get. 'Has the coroner indicated when he will release the body for burial?'

'I don't think so', Tim replied in a worried tone. 'I gather the pathologist is still examining certain organs to establish whether David Anderson may have been drugged beforehand.'

'Oh, I do hope so', Alison broke in. 'It's too awful to contemplate otherwise. I've had nightmares every night since his poor body was discovered.' She quickly began to write and Margaret Lakington wondered whether her nightmares were destined to become part of the minutes.

'Just make a note that the meeting approved the sending of a wreath', Sir Wesley said quickly. 'There's no need for anything else.' Addressing the assembled company he went on, 'I suggest a donation of one pound fifty per head should be sufficient for the purchase of an appropriate wreath and we'll leave it to you, Miss Tremlett, to collect the money.'

'Do you want to contribute, Tim?' she asked. 'Even though you're not normally a resident?'

An annoyed frown gathered on Sir Wesley's brow as always happened when he felt the chair was being bypassed. Before he could say anything, however, Tim Moxon spoke.

'Mr Goran and the management will be sending their own wreaths.'

'Does it have to be a wreath?' Margaret asked. 'I'd much sooner my money went on a spray of flowers.'

There were nods and a general murmur of assent.

'Those in favour of a floral spray instead of a wreath', Sir Wesley said quickly before further conversation could break out. Hands went up. 'That's settled then.' He turned towards Tim. 'Now, Mr Moxon, perhaps you'd be so good as to give us a progress report. I assume the police have given you some idea what they are up to and, more importantly, to what extent their continuing enquiries are likely to disrupt our lives here.'

'They'll be disrupted all right if one of us is arrested', Doug Potter remarked. 'No need for you all to look shocked. I'm sure I'm only voicing a thought that's going through all our minds.' He turned to Margaret, who was sitting next to him. 'I know you think it must have been an inside job.' His glance went round the room. 'So the odds are we have a murderer with us in this room.'

If anyone had interrupted his court in such an outrageous fashion, Sir Wesley would have had no hesitation in committing him to the cells for contempt, and his expression left none of those present in any doubt that he wished he still had that power. Out of the corner of his eye he noticed Alison Tremlett scribbling hard.

'We don't need that most unwarranted remark recorded in the minutes', he said savagely.

'You can stick it in as far as I'm concerned, Alison', Doug said. 'You know me; I've always called a spade a spade.'

'We don't want this meeting to degenerate into a slanging match', Sir Wesley said in his most disdainfully judicial voice.

'You're not in your court now, Sir Wesley', Doug observed. 'This is meant to be a democratic meeting and I've as much right to air my views as anyone else. And as for a slanging match, who slung first?'

It was John Dixon who broke the tension this brisk exchange had caused.

'May I suggest, Mr Chairman, that Tim Moxon be asked to tell us anything we all ought to know and that the meeting then be adjourned?'

'I support that', Margaret said firmly. Mrs Potter and Lady Binfield added quick nods, as did the Unterbys who had begun to wish they had remained on holiday.

'Very well', Sir Wesley said in an icy tone. 'Perhaps you'd be so good as to comply with the meeting's wish,

82

Mr Moxon.'

'I'm afraid there's very little I can tell you', Tim said in a distinctly apprehensive tone. 'It's almost certain the police will want to question everyone further, so you must expect to have them around for quite a while. However, I'm sure they'll be as tactful as they can be.' He paused. 'And that's about all, I think.'

'Have the police found out what young Anderson was doing in the apartment below this one?' Doug Potter threw Sir Wesley an unpleasant look. 'And how he got into it? That's what I'd like to know.'

'They think he must have had a key', Tim replied uncomfortably. 'It was one of the apartments he looked over before he decided on the one he eventually bought. He could have had the key copied', Tim concluded vaguely.

'And what was he doing there?' Doug persisted. 'Who has a theory about that? What about you, Sir Wesley? After all, his body was found up the chimney that joins yours. It strikes me he may have been trying to—'

'—Trying to what?' Sir Wesley broke in angrily. 'You're talking offensive rubbish. I declare the meeting closed.' Suiting action to words, he pushed back his chair and stood up.

'At least we'll be back for that programme', Desmond Murray remarked to his friend, as they prepared to leave.

'What programme's that?' Margaret enquired.

Desmond gave her a wry smile. 'A documentary on gay rights', he said.

'Tell me', Margaret said, lowering her voice, 'do you think David Anderson was gay?'

Desmond raised his eyebrows in mock surprise. 'It takes one to know one, is that why you're asking us?' Then in a more serious tone he said, 'My impression was that David was totally uninterested in sex.'

John Dixon nodded. 'I agree with Des. There are such people.'

'I know', Margaret retorted drily. 'I had the misfortune to marry one. My first husband was only interested in making money. He regarded sex as a tiresome distraction.' She smiled. 'Anyway, I hope you enjoy your programme. I think I may watch it, too.'

When she got back to her apartment, however, she decided that, much as she disliked the telephone, she must call Rosa and give her an account of the evening's events.

'Of course, one always knew that there was no love lost between them', she said as she reached the end of her recital, 'but this evening the daggers were really drawn. Except that Doug Potter's instrument was more a sledgehammer.' She went on in a husky voice, 'It seems that David Anderson's death is going to have as many repercussions as a political scandal. But perhaps that was only to be expected.'

'I don't see why', Rosa said thoughtfully.

'See what, dear?'

'Why his death should necessarily set neighbour against neighbour.'

'It's not death so much as the mode of his demise that's turning us into a lot of dangerous animals.'

'It's obvious that Doug Potter came to the meeting determined to needle Sir Wesley. I wonder why he chose to do it in such a public fashion.'

'Because he's a tough, ruthless man.'

'I thought you rather liked him.'

'I do, but not because I think he hides a heart of gold.'

Rosa was silent as she considered what her godmother had told her. She was aware that Sir Wesley knew things about Doug Potter that nobody else at Deepwood Grange knew. Matters on which he had sought to enlist her help. The question was, did Doug Potter have anything on the ex-judge? Be that as it may she was now more certain than ever that Robin had given her sound advice regarding what could only be seen as a vendetta between Sir Wesley and his one-time client.

'How did John and Desmond react to all this?' she asked.

'They were as embarrassed as the rest of us. Sally Binfield was the person I was most sorry for. Made worse by the fact it all happened in her own apartment. She couldn't even walk out.' She paused and went on, 'Who was that god in Wagner's *Ring*? Wotan, wasn't it? Spends his time trying to retain his dignity after he's lost his authority. Just like Sir Wesley this evening.'

'What about Thelma Potter?'

'She just sat there with an innocent expression. I suspect Thelma has learnt when to say her piece and when to stay silent.'

'Whatever else, it must have provided good copy for Alison', Rosa remarked.

'There's something about that woman I can't like, Rosa. It's nothing to do with her nauseating books. But I think she's a phoney.'

'In what way?'

'She pretends to be terribly upset by what's happened, but, if you ask me, she'd be as capable of committing cold-blooded murder as anyone.'

CHAPTER 10

Earlier that same day Detective Chief Inspector James had driven back to London, having first delivered his sons at school and exchanged a friendly word with one of

Paul's teachers at the entrance.

Before leaving town the previous evening he had made contact with the nearest police station to Osming Street and been delighted to discover that one of its uniformed inspectors was someone with whom he had struck up a friendship on a police training course. Inspector Pilley wasn't on duty at that moment, he was told, but would be on night shift if he cared to call back later.

'Hello, Colin, it's David James', he said when he telephoned the station from home around eleven o'clock that evening.

'I was only thinking of you a few days ago, David, and reminding myself to let you know that I'd left the Yard and been posted to the outback of Bayswater. I feel I'm a policeman again. Sitting on my backside in 'A' Department at the Yard was not my idea of police work. Anyway, what can I do for you, David?'

CI James told him.

'No problem at all', Inspector Pilley said immediately. 'I happen to know one of the partners of Crane & Co. I'll speak to him first thing in the morning and say we need to get into Anderson's flat and that he ought to be present, at least when we enter. What time do you suggest?'

'Can we meet at Osming Street at eleven?'

'Suits me.'

'Do you think the agents will have a key?'

'I've no idea, but I'm sure we'll be able to gain entry one way or another. If necessary, we'll get a locksmith.'

As things turned out the attendance of a locksmith did become a necessity, the front-door lock on Flat 6 having defeated Mr Duckworth of Crane & Co, who arrived armed with a formidable set of keys, as well as the less orthodox attentions of Inspector Pilley and CI James. They retired to the pub across the road while the locksmith was sent for and it then took the best part of an hour to get the door open.

'It's one of those new German locks', he kept on murmuring as he worked away, watched by the other three. 'Take a bit of time they do. Nothing brittle or flimsy about them', he went on, matching action with running commentary.

Finally the door was opened and they went in. At first sight it appeared to be functionally furnished and James wondered why such a sophisticated lock had been fitted. Apart from a video recorder and some hi-fi equipment, there appeared to be little that would appeal to a burglar. In one corner of the living room was a desk and James went over and began to open its drawers. In the bottom one were four Citizens' Band two-way radio sets, and in the one above two Japanese cameras, one with a telescopic lens attachment, the other with a self-developing mechanism. James assumed that the two-way radios and the cameras fell within Anderson's tools of trade. The next drawer he opened revealed a number of bugging devices.

'Is this the sort of stuff you were expecting to find, David?' Inspector Pilley asked.

'I'd no idea what I'd find. But obviously investigation was the name of his game.'

'I'd have thought he might have needed this stuff with him.'

'I'm sure he had similar items down there, but that they were all removed by whoever killed him.'

At that moment the telephone began to ring. It was situated on top of the desk next to a large, ivory Buddha. The three men exchanged wary glances.

'You'd better answer it', Inspector Pilley said.

'Hello', James said in a slightly husky voice as he lifted the receiver.

'David?'

'Yes.'

87

'It's Peter, David. I've just got back. I'm still at the airport. I wasn't sure where you'd be, but thought I'd try Osming Street for a start. Will you be there all the afternoon? If so, I'll come round.'

'Yes, I'll be here.'

'Has something happened, David? You sound a bit off.'

'I'll tell you when I see you.'

'Who's going to win the two o'clock?' the man called Peter asked abruptly.

'I'm sorry, I didn't quite catch that—'

'—Who are you? Where's David?' the voice demanded anxiously.

'I'm Detective Chief Inspector James of the Sussex police. Will you please tell me your name? I need to meet you.' He began to say something further when the line went dead. 'Damn! As soon as he realised it wasn't Anderson, he rang off.'

'Sounds like he has a guilty conscience', Inspector Pilley observed. 'Any hope of tracing him?'

CI James shook his head. 'Somebody called Peter phoning from an airport. Hardly enough for a quick identification. I wonder if there's an address book anywhere in the flat.'

'Much more likely he had it with him at Deepwood Grange.'

'I know. In which case it was removed by the murderer with all the other personal data. Trouble is that whoever killed Anderson had a ten days' start on us. Ten days while Anderson's body lay undiscovered up the chimney.'

The thoughtful silence which followed was broken by a sudden angry exclamation from the doorway.

'What the hell's going on here?'

The three men turned to find a girl staring imperiously at them. She must have been over six feet tall and had a smooth, coffee-cream complexion. Her features were beautifully moulded and her physique was that of a medal-winning athlete. She was wearing a black trouser suit whose creases were as sharp as her manner.

'Who the hell are you?' she asked, without any trace of fear.

'I'm Detective Chief Inspector James. I'm in charge of enquiries into David Anderson's death. Who are you?'

'David dead?' she said disbelievingly. 'So that's why I couldn't get in touch with him! What happened?'

'Who are you?' James repeated.

'I'm Wanda Velasquez. I'm his secretary. I've been away and only came back yesterday. I tried to phone David at Deepwood Grange last night and again this morning, but couldn't get any answer. Then I phoned here, but again no reply, so I decided to come round and see if he'd left any message for me. I assumed he'd gone abroad on business at short notice. Now you say he's dead. . . .'

'Where've you been these past two weeks?'

'In Trinidad visiting my family. I was born there. I've been away a month. David said it would be a good time to go while he was tied up at Deepwood Grange.'

'Tied up doing what?'

The girl frowned. 'He was investigating a diamond robbery', she said hesitantly.

'On whose behalf?'

'The insurers.'

'Are you saying that he suspected someone at Deepwood Grange as having been involved in the robbery?'

'Yes.'

'Who?'

'I don't know.'

'I don't believe you.'

She gave a shrug of indifference. 'It's still the truth. When he was hot on the trail in a sensitive investigation he never told me or anyone else a thing. He always used to say it was safer not to put anything in writing or share a secret.'

'Even so, you must have had some idea', James said in a tone half-coaxing, half-demanding.

'I didn't because I had no need to.'

'How long have you worked for David Anderson?'

'Just over a year.'

'This diamond robbery you mentioned, did the police make any arrests?'

'They picked up some of the smaller fry, but the big boys got away. They usually do, don't they?' she added in a taunting voice.

'Who were the insurers?' James asked, refusing to rise.

'A Dutch firm.'

'Why Dutch?'

'Because the diamonds were owned by a Dutch dealer. They were in London, but destined for Hong Kong.'

'You seem to know quite a lot about the case.'

'But I still don't know whom David was on to', she said with a touch of impatience.

'Supposing I tell you the names of the residents at Deepwood Grange, might that help your memory?'

'I have them on file in the office', she said dismissively. 'And there's nothing wrong with my memory. David always held his cards close to his chest in delicate operations.'

'I'd like to examine your office files', James said after a thoughtful pause.

'I'd need legal advice first.'

'Even though your employer has been murdered in the course of one of his investigations?'

'Murdered! Even so, co-operation with the police isn't everything.'

'I don't understand you', James said in a tone which was a blend of bewilderment and irritation.

'That's too bad!'

'Where is your office?' he asked, swallowing his exasperation.

'13 Dyke Street. It's near Fenchurch Street Station.'

'OK to go there now?'

'Yes, if you want to', she said after a second's hesitation.

It was on their way in a taxi that he told her the full circumstances of David Anderson's death. Beyond a quick grimace she made no comment.

Meanwhile Inspector Pilley had left Osming Street to return to his station and Mr Duckworth to his office to make up for a profitless morning.

'You didn't show as much surprise as I expected when I told you Anderson had been murdered', James now remarked, watching her closely.

'I'm not easily surprised. And anyway I'd guessed', she said coldly.

'Did you think he might be in some danger?'

'He accepted danger as part of the job, just like an oil-rig diver does.'

'Do you know anything about his will?'

'No.'

'Who holds it?'

'His lawyer, I imagine.'

'Who's that?'

'His name's Peter Chen. He's half Chinese. David knew him from his boyhood days in Hong Kong.' She smiled. 'He's not your ordinary sort of lawyer.'

'Has he been abroad recently?'

'Could be. He travels around a good deal. Why?'

'Somebody called Peter phoned just before you arrived at Osming Street. Said he was at the airport. He rang off abruptly when he realised I wasn't David Anderson.'

'It could have been Peter Chen', she remarked with a nod.

'Where's his office?'

'In Battersea. He works from home. He's very rich and picks and chooses what he'll do. At the same time he's a very able lawyer.'

'Who looks after his office when he's on his travels?'

'He has an assistant, Paula Kinney. But she's away at the moment having a baby.'

David James felt as if he was caught in a maze. Every turn seemed to lead him into another cul-de-sac.

'He doesn't sound a very satisfactory sort of lawyer', he said, a trifle peevishly.

'He was perfect for David. They understood and respected each other's ways.'

'I'll call him from your office', James said in a determined voice.

Wanda Velasquez's only comment was to turn her head and gaze out of the taxi window.

Dyke Street was a short, narrow, one-way street joining two major thoroughfares. No 13 was about half-way along it on the left, a grime ingrained, three storey building. When the taxi pulled up, Wanda got out and stalked inside, leaving CI James to pay the fare. Although he had expected to do so, her manner made him feel as if he was an unwanted suitor.

She was waiting for him inside by a small, antiquated lift.

'We're on the second floor', she said, and stood back so that he could press the button.

As they stepped out, he noticed that the door straight ahead of them had 'Anderson Associates' on its frosted glass panel. Beneath in small letters was written 'Investigation Specialists'.

'Looks as if it'd be easier to break into his office than his flat', James observed as Wanda produced a bunch of keys.

'Don't be fooled by impressions! That's no ordinary

glass panel. It's resisted tougher onslaughts than the police could mount.'

'Why did he need all this protection for his home and his office?'

'Because he operated in a dangerous and competitive world. One in which no holds were barred.' They were standing in a small office which contained a desk, a steel filing cabinet and a formidable looking safe in a corner behind the door. 'This is David's office. Now you're here, what do you want?'

Her tone was aggressive and James was thoughtful for a moment. Then he said, 'Why don't you put the kettle on and make us a cup of coffee?'

'All right, if you want one.'

He followed her out to a small pantry which contained a sink, a refrigerator and an electric kettle. She opened a wall cupboard and took out two mugs and a jar of instant coffee.

'What are you going to do now?' he asked as she reached into the refrigerator for a carton of milk.

'Make coffee. Isn't that what you wanted?'

'That's not what I meant, as you're bright enough to know. But let me ask you something else first. Why are you so hostile?'

'Because I don't like the police', she said, without looking round.

'Is that as a result of some personal experience?'

'A family experience, let's say.'

'In this country?'

'No.'

'In Trinidad?'

'Yes.'

'It's not fair to judge the police here by those in another country.'

'Isn't it?' She turned round and handed him a mug. 'Help yourself to sugar.'

'Who was involved? Your father?'

'No.'

'Who then?'

'My youngest brother if you must know. He's nineteen.'

'What happened to him?'

'He was sent to prison for six months for allegedly assaulting a police officer. The case was a total frame-up. But as a result he was thrown out of college and now he's working in the crappy kitchen of a crappy hotel.' Her voice was full of bitterness.

'I'm sorry about your brother, but the British police can hardly be blamed for his plight.'

'The officer who framed him, Inspector Santos by name, had just returned from a course in the UK where he'd doubtless been taught how to keep the natives in their place. He's the most arrogant man I've ever met.'

'Were you home then when all this happened?'

'No, but I made a point of meeting him when I was there last month. I told him I hoped he would end up in the gutter where he belonged.'

CI James gazed at her with a mixture of awe and respect.

'I need your co-operation Miss Velasquez', he said after a while. 'Moreover, I don't think you have any right to withhold it. You worked for David Anderson; you're not the appointed guardian of his affairs. Let me remind you again, I'm investigating a particularly callous and brutal murder. Now, I'd like to see the file relating to the matter which took him to Deepwood Grange.'

'It won't assist you.'

'That's for me to judge.'

She went over to the safe and made sure that CI James couldn't see what she was doing to open it. She suddenly turned her head and gave him a frustrated glare.

'It won't open. Somebody's changed the combination.'

'Somebody?'

'It must have been David while I was away.' Observing his sceptical expression she went on with a touch of impatience, 'He used to change it from time to time and let me know, but because I've been away he never had a chance to tell me.'

'Would he have written it down somewhere?'

'He always memorised it, and I had to as well.'

'Was there any sign of anyone having been in here while you were away?'

'I don't think so', she said cautiously. 'Anyway, I imagine David came in a few times. He must have done to collect mail.'

James wondered who else had been in for a leisurely snoop. The murderer had certainly had an opportunity of doing so. All those missing keys from Anderson's apartment. His killer must still have them.

They were still staring at the defiant safe when the phone began to ring.

'Answer it', he said as he followed her out of the room into a tiny adjoining one.

She lifted the receiver and gave her number in a wary tone.

'Oh, it's you, Peter', she exclaimed, as James grabbed the phone from her.

'Mr Chen, this is Detective Chief Inspector James once more. You'd better come over to Mr Anderson's office immediately.'

'Why, what's happened? Where's David?'

'He's dead. Murdered. If you want to know more, get here quickly.'

'Are you being serious?'

'Yes.'

'How did he die?'

'Just get on over here and stop asking questions.'

Peter Chen arrived twenty-five minutes later. He had a smooth, round face and looked absurdly young for a solicitor, even a half-Chinese one. He was wearing a black corduroy suit and a white roll-top sweater. He gave Wanda a kiss on the cheek and without waiting for an invitation sat down at David Anderson's desk.

'This is terrible news about David', he said. 'What happened?'

He listened in silence while CI James gave him the facts.

'When did you last see him?' James asked at the end.

Chen pursed his lips. 'It could only have been a few days before his death from what you've said. We had lunch at my flat the day before I left for Hong Kong, which was October the thirty-first.'

'Were you in Hong Kong all the time you were away?'

'No. I was there five days and then flew on to the States. I had business in Los Angeles and Washington. I flew back from there last night.'

'Was any of your business to do with David?'

'No.'

'When you saw him just before you left did he mention his investigation at Deepwood Grange?'

'He merely said he was hopeful of cracking the nut. He thought he now knew who was behind the diamond robbery he was interested in.'

'Did he say who it was?'

'No.'

'Or give any hint?'

'Not really. David didn't believe in confiding in others. He was always very much his own man.'

'You said "not really". Did he say anything at all that could help me find his murderer?'

'He said, in passing, that if his suspicions proved well founded, there was a touch of irony about the whole matter.'

'A touch of irony? Did he say what he meant by that?'

'No. And I didn't press him.'

'Pity.'

'It wouldn't have produced anything more if I had. David never divulged anything unless he wanted to. And he rarely felt the need to.'

'I understand you hold his will?'

'Yes.'

'Who benefits under it?'

'He left everything to his step-sister who lives in Australia.'

'I understood he was an only child.'

'His parents adopted a little girl when David was about eight and had come to school in this country.'

'Are you ever in touch with her?'

Peter Chen gave a sad little smile. 'She's married to my brother.'

'I wonder why David's bank manager thought he was an only child', James remarked with a slight frown.

Chen let out a sudden giggle. 'David hated being asked questions about himself and he always found Mr Saunders a bit nosey. He probably told him he was an only child to forestall further questions, particularly as his step-sister is Chinese.' Observing James's expression he added, 'It's all quite simple, Chief Inspector, David's parents adopted a Chinese orphan who became David's step-sister and is now my sister-in-law.'

'Thank you for that careful explanation', James remarked drily. 'I take it that you will notify David's parents of his death?'

His demeanour became immediately cast down. 'I'll call them tonight. Actually, David's mother is seriously ill. She had a heart attack soon after I'd seen her in Hong Kong. It's not certain that she will live.'

'Will his father come home?'

'Home? Hong Kong's his home. He told me he was

confident of dying before 1997.'

'Are they wealthy people?'

'Not by Hong Kong standards of wealth, but they're not poor.'

'What'll happen to the business now?' James asked, glancing round the tiny office.

Chen gave a graphic shrug.

'It dies with David. He was the business.' He glanced towards Wanda. 'You'd better come and work for me, sweetheart. I don't fancy having Paula changing nappies in the office.'

CI James reflected somewhat ruefully that he had learnt a lot about David Anderson in the past couple of hours without getting any nearer to knowing who had murdered him.

'I will come down to Deepwood Grange and help you find the murderer', Chen now said, with the sort of confidence displayed by Hercule Poirot in his heyday.

CHAPTER 11

Rosa decided that she should phone Sir Wesley, rather than write and say she was unable to fulfil his commission. She felt it would be more courteous, not to say more placatory.

It was late afternoon on the day after the residents' meeting that she chose to make her call.

Lady Binfield answered the phone and she and Rosa exchanged a few obligatory comments on the weather before she fetched her husband.

'Yes, Miss Epton,' he said immediately he picked up

the receiver, 'what have you been able to find out for me?'

'Nothing, I'm afraid.' The silence at the other end became heavy as she went on, 'My contact at the Yard is away and I'm not going to be able to help you.'

'I see', he said in a tone of unmistakable displeasure. 'I was relying on you to find something out about the person we've discussed. I don't know whether you've spoken to your godmother today, but we had an emergency meeting of the residents' association last night and his behaviour was quite disgraceful. He flaunted his brazenness and I'm more than ever sure he was in some way involved in Anderson's death.'

'Why don't you speak to Detective Chief Inspector James? He seems an efficient, level-headed officer and I'm sure he'd respect your confidence.' She refrained from adding that even retired high court judges carried a certain amount of clout, deciding that Sir Wesley was not in the mood to be amused by such an observation.

As it was, Sir Wesley was silent for a time before continuing in a sombre tone, 'I suspect that Anderson was involved with Potter in some criminal activity and got killed for his pains.'

'What sort of criminal activity?' Rosa asked.

'There's no shortage, Miss Epton. Hardly a month goes by without some gang or other netting a haul that runs into millions. Those sort of crimes need capital to set them up, not to mention skilled planning and execution. You know as well as I do that criminal enterprise these days is developing as fast as modern technology.'

'Yes, I know', Rosa said. 'Though most of my clients still seem to belong to the steam age. That's why they get caught, of course.'

'Which protects society and provides you with a living', Sir Wesley remarked sardonically.

'Once the police have successfully probed David Anderson's background, they should be well on their way to solving his murder', Rosa said, breaking the silence that followed Sir Wesley's previous observation.

'It should lead them straight to Potter', Sir Wesley remarked and a moment later rang off with a gruff goodbye.

Rosa was still puzzled by his apparent reluctance to tell the police what he knew about Doug Potter. It wasn't as if he entertained any doubts that he was the same man who had stood trial for a vicious murder fifty years before.

When she arrived home that evening she followed her usual practice of having a long, hot bath, after which she retired to her tiny kitchen with a drink to prepare supper. She enjoyed cooking and found it therapeutic after a day spent in court or the office. Cooking just for herself could sometimes be a chore, but she invariably made herself do so and only when she was exceptionally tired would she take something out of the freezer and pop it in the oven, letting the automatic timer tell her when she could eat.

On this particular evening she had brought home some fillets of Dover sole which she planned to cook in a cheese sauce and garnish with asparagus tips. Once a week an enterprising young man came down Whitford Street selling fresh fish from his van. As soon as his familiar cry was heard Stephanie would dash out and buy for Rosa and herself. Ever since Rosa had successfully defended him on a charge of obstruction, he had regarded everyone working at 12 Whitford Street as deserving only the finest of what he had to offer.

After preparing her meal and putting it into the oven, she freshened her drink – vodka and pure orange juice – and went into the living room where she switched on the television. She regarded it as a period of total relaxation and refused to desecrate it by opening her briefcase and taking out papers. It was better, if need be, to stay up an extra forty-five minutes at the end of the day.

She watched the start of the evening news, then decided she could manage without the world's problems and switched off. Almost immediately her mind turned to events at Deepwood Grange. Her natural curiosity had been aroused by what had happened there and she felt she should be able to apply her deductive faculty more profitably than she had done. After all, there wasn't a profusion of suspects. Indeed there were very few who could be so regarded in any serious light.

Her godmother had certainly had nothing to do with the murder, nor could she regard Alison Tremlett as a serious suspect, despite what Margaret had recently said about her. Apart from any other consideration she would have been physically incapable of stuffing somebody twice her own size up a chimney; and there was no evidence that she had had an accomplice.

As for Sir Wesley Binfield, Rosa's natural instinct was to dismiss him as a suspect. She just couldn't accept that judges went around committing gang-type murders. Some might be tempted to kill their wives, but that was different. In any event what possible motive could he have had? A judge with something disreputable in his background might be open to blackmail, but that hardly applied to a retired judge living in the country.

So, who was left? Doug Potter and the two gays. Rosa was loath to think that John Dixon and Desmond Murray might be murderers. Though she scarcely knew them, she liked them, especially Desmond whom she had found a most engaging person. She realised, however, that she knew only what they had told her about themselves. That John had been an interior designer and Desmond had been in catering, and that they owned a restaurant in the area. Though they were closer in age to David Anderson than the other residents, they hadn't

MICHAEL UNDERWOOD

given the impression of knowing him any better. There
was certainly no suggestion that David's arrival at
Deepwood Grange had caused a rift in their life. On the
contrary, John and Desmond seemed to enjoy a relaxed
and stable relationship. Considerably more so than
many gay couples she knew.

Thus it came down to Doug Potter to fill the number
one spot for prime suspect. Rosa would have put murder
within his capabilities, even without Sir Wesley's startling disclosure about the past. It was, of course, possible
that his wealth had been hard earned, but it could easily
have been acquired in ways less legitimate. If David
Anderson had been secretly stalking Doug Potter, he
could have given himself away and paid the penalty. But
that raised the question, on whose behalf was Anderson
doing the stalking? Rosa decided there were several
answers to that. It might have been a rival crime chief
whom Doug had cheated. It might even have been an
undercover job on behalf of a newspaper out for a major
scoop. But most likely, she thought, he had been
undertaking a private eye job for one of Doug Potter's
victims.

Appetising smells were coming from the kitchen and
she got up from her chair, her mind still on events at
Deepwood Grange rather than her supper.

And where, she wondered, did Tim Moxon fit in? He
had seemed worried and anxious even before the murder.
She was sure that he was more involved than anyone
knew.

She let out a sigh. So long as she remained on the
outside there was little she could do to satisfy her
investigative curiosity. What was needed was for someone to be charged with murder and to engage her
professionally! But what a callous and macabre wish that
was! And, of course, she didn't really mean it. Moreover,
there was nobody at Deepwood Grange whom she would

102

particularly like to have as a client, Desmond Murray excepted. And she certainly didn't want to see him arrested just for her benefit.

But, in fact, her deeper involvement in the case was to come about in an entirely unexpected way.

CHAPTER 12

By a coincidence of which neither was aware, Aldo Goran was also dining off fillet of sole that evening. According to the menu his was called *Fillets of sole en surprise*. It too had a cheese flavour, but additionally contained various ingredients unknown to Rosa's less sophisticated larder. He was eating it in his favourite London restaurant, which also happened to be one of the capital's most expensive.

He sat alone at a secluded corner table and sipped from time to time at a glass of chilled Chablis.

He had never greatly cared for London, preferring Paris, where he had a flat, and even Rome and Madrid. He regarded London as a working city and not a place he visited for pleasure. Nevertheless, he held a UK passport, as well as a Swiss resident's permit, and had never considered exchanging his nationality for any other.

When probed about his origins he would reply blandly that he had some of the blood of every country that bordered the Mediterranean running through his veins.

He had been born in Sardinia forty-two years ago of an Italian mother and a half-Egyptian father. His father's other half was a confusing racial cocktail.

He had been brought up in Marseilles where his father had met a violent death when Aldo was seven. His

103

mother then moved to London with an English truck driver, who very soon deserted her and Aldo. He recalled his early years in England with hatred. It was a life of constant harassment and running battles with various authorities, with only a fierce determination to survive sustaining him from day to day. When he was fifteen his mother died and Aldo was on his own.

Now, twenty-seven years later, he always stayed in the best suites of Europe's top hotels and dined at the most exclusive restaurants. He had never doubted that it would be so once he had cast off the shackles of his background. With homes in Geneva and Paris and property interests all over the world, he was a millionaire several times over.

But no investment had given him greater personal satisfaction than the purchase of Deepwood Grange in lush, green Sussex. It wasn't that he hankered after the life of a country gentleman, but the acquisition of an English country mansion represented triumph over his past and a settling of untold scores with the authorities of his youth.

And now something had happened at Deepwood Grange to anger him. He had always done his best to avoid unnecessary trouble simply because it consumed time and energy more profitably employed elsewhere. But trouble with a vengeance had broken out there.

He had personally vetted the credentials of everyone buying an apartment at Deepwood Grange and had taken an interest in its residents beyond the normal. Indeed, they might sleep a trifle uneasily if they ever became aware how much he knew about each of them.

Tim Moxon had been his trusted intermediary and all the evidence was that Tim had let him down. That was why he hadn't let him know he was coming to London.

He was brooding over the situation that had arisen when a waiter brought the lemon sorbet he had ordered.

Though he didn't have any tendency to put on weight, he still kept a close watch on his figure. He had been vain about his personal appearance ever since he had bought his first suit.

Two cups of coffee later he signed his bill and was bowed out by waiters and maitre d'hôtel alike.

'Who was that?' a fellow diner who was eating there for the first time enquired with curiosity as he watched him depart.

'Mr Aldo Goran', the maitre d'hôtel said in a tone of chilly politeness.

'Never heard of him. Is he famous?'

'Dining here bestows its own fame', the maitre d' replied haughtily, and swept away.

When he got back to his hotel suite, Aldo Goran sat in an armchair and continued his brooding over what had brought him to London. Later he would probably go to a casino for an hour or two. He enjoyed roulette and was a controlled and therefore often successful gambler. It had become one of his main pleasures in life since he had given up women. Three wives had been three too many. Now if he needed a girl, there was never any problem in finding one, but serious entanglements were to be sedulously avoided.

He rose from his chair and went over to unlock the black leather document case which lay on the desk. He removed a slim folder and returned to his chair. The folder bore no legend on its outside, but contained personal details of the residents of Deepwood Grange.

There was one particular sheet that held his attention.

CHAPTER 13

Margaret Lakington had been a bad sleeper for the past twenty years. More often than not the small hours would find her reading or listening to a quietly tuned radio.

Sleeplessness no longer bothered her; it was something with which she had come to terms. As she said, she didn't have to get up in the morning and go off to work, so what did it matter? She didn't even take sleeping tablets any longer. She regarded the condition philosophically and as a very minor affliction for somebody her age.

Two nights after the residents' association meeting, she awoke around half past two and knew from experience that she had little expectation of further sleep before dawn. Propping herself up against the pillows, she reached for her book. Jane Austen was her favourite night-hour reading and she was currently about halfway through *Mansfield Park*. She reckoned to read each of the author's books once a year.

She had read only a couple of pages when she thought she heard sounds coming from the Great Hall. It was more furtive than the noise made by someone returning home late and yet she couldn't properly define the sounds that reached her ears. If it had not been for recent events, she wouldn't have taken any further notice. As it was, however, her senses were immediately alert.

For a minute she lay back listening intently, still holding her book. Then with growing curiosity she got out of bed and went across to the window. The whole house appeared to be in darkness, but by twisting her head she was able to see lights on in Tim Moxon's apartment over the stables. It showed round the edges of the drawn curtains.

She hadn't been aware that Tim was down, but his comings and goings were his own affair and the residents often knew of his presence only if they happened to bump into him.

She was about to get back into bed when she again heard indistinct sounds coming from below. Pulling on her thick wool dressing gown and tying a scarf over her head she went to her front door and opened it. The gallery and Great Hall were in total darkness and no further sound reached her ears. For half a minute she stood there listening while her eyes grew accustomed to the darkness which was relieved by a pale suffusion of light filtered through the glass roof.

Quite suddenly there was a rustling sound accompanied by a faint moan from somewhere over by the inner entrance door.

Wrapping her dressing gown more tightly about her she moved to the top of the staircase where she paused to listen again. By now she was able to make out the outline of various objects in the Great Hall. She had no feeling of fear, merely of great curiosity. Something was not as it should be and she, Margaret Lakington, was going to find out what was amiss. She had once tackled and put to flight a night intruder in her home in South Africa and so wasn't easily alarmed.

Moving slowly and cautiously she set off downstairs, then, hugging the perimeter of the Great Hall, she made her way round to the front door. She had just reached it when her foot struck something soft. At the same time a groan came from the floor and a body rolled against her legs. The next moment a torch beam shone up into her face and she jerked her head back with shock.

'So it was you, Margaret', a voice said accusingly.

107

'Why did you do it?'

'Is that you, Alison?'

'You know it's me. Why did you do it?'

'Do what?'

'Hit me over the head, of course. I thought it was you just before I passed out. How long have I been here?'

'I've no idea. I heard noises and came down to investigate. I nearly tripped over your body.'

'I suppose you're bound to deny it', Alison said in a long-suffering tone. 'I know you've never liked me, but you didn't have to try and kill me.'

'You don't know what you're saying, Alison. You're obviously concussed. I'll help you back to your apartment and phone for the doctor.'

'What time is it?'

'Between half past two and three.'

Alison had laid the torch on the floor beside her and Margaret could see that she was wearing the voluminous purple velvet cloak that hung from her shoulders to her feet.

'My head aches', Alison said, as Margaret bent down to help her to her feet. 'Did you really intend to kill me?' she went on in a matter-of-fact tone.

'I've not touched you', Margaret said sharply. 'Here, take my arm.'

'How do I know you won't make a further attempt when you get me into my apartment?'

'If that thought is troubling you, you can find your own way across the Great Hall.'

Alison rose slowly to her feet, holding on to Margaret for support.

'We mustn't wake up any of the others', she said in a sly tone. 'I'd have to tell them that you attacked me.'

Margaret forebore to reply. Her threshold of impatience was low at the best of times and she felt herself sorely tried. Equally she had no wish to provoke Alison into further crazy fantasies. With luck she would wake up in the morning with a more lucid mind, though Margaret was beginning to wonder whether she had ever possessed such a faculty.

'Where exactly were you struck?' she asked.

'You should know, Margaret.'

Biting back any comment, she ran her hand over the back of Alison's head. There didn't appear to be any bleeding.

'You know quite well where you hit me', Alison said, focusing the beam of the torch on to the left side of her face where Margaret saw a large, purple bruise over the temple. 'What have you done with the weapon?' she enquired.

'For the last time, Alison, I never attacked you. Maybe you'd care to say what you were doing at this hour of the night?'

'I'd been visiting a friend', Alison said guilelessly.

'And where were you attacked?'

'I was just coming through the front door. There was a sudden movement that startled me and then I realised it was you standing there.'

'Hold on to my arm', Margaret said with exemplary forebearance, 'and we'll go across to your apartment. Have you got your key?'

Alison reached into the pocket of her cape and produced it. On reaching her door, Margaret opened it and steered her inside.

'Get into bed and I'll fetch you a drink. Do you have any brandy? Or perhaps a glass of hot milk would be better. Then you can say if you want me to send for the doctor.'

Alison slipped off her cape to reveal a black negligée beneath. Margaret gave her a startled look. So it was that sort of visit she'd been making! The nearest apartment to where Margaret had found her was John and Desmond's, but she couldn't envisage them playing host to the female apparition standing before her.

'Hurry up and get into bed', she said firmly as she went off to the kitchen to make Alison a hot drink. Brandy, she decided, might make her behave more oddly than ever.

When she returned to the bedroom, Alison was gazing at herself in a mirror and delicately fingering her bruised temple.

'I'd better get you something for that', Margaret remarked, and went off to search the bathroom cupboard. She found a bottle of old-fashioned witch-hazel. At least that wouldn't do her any harm, even if it didn't do her much good either.

Returning to the bedroom, she dabbed the lotion on Alison's bruise.

'Shall I call the doctor?'

'No.' Alison sounded suddenly subdued and sleepy.

'Nevertheless, I strongly advise you to see him later today. Head injuries can produce strange effects. Is there anything else I can do for you before I go back to my own bed?'

Alison shook her head and Margaret left, closing the bedroom door behind her. As she walked past the slip of a room that Alison used as a study, she observed a pile of manuscript. Griselda Falcon had obviously been hard at work and had succeeded in giving her alter ego an overheated imagination.

As she got back into bed she noticed from her watch that barely half an hour had passed since she had gone off to investigate. It seemed more like a lifetime. It was remarkable, too, that nobody else had appeared on the scene. They were clearly better sleepers than she.

Before returning to her bed she had gone to the window and looked out. Tim Moxon's apartment was now in darkness.

Around six o'clock she dozed off to sleep, but was wide

awake again forty-five minutes later. It was time to phone Rosa. A sleepy voice answered.

'Sorry if I woke you up, my dear, but I must talk to you. Are you sufficiently awake to listen?'

'Yes, go ahead', Rosa said with a feeling of foreboding. Days that began with telephone calls at 7 a.m. usually went from bad to worse.

By the time Margaret finished her recital of what had happened, Rosa was fully awake.

'What an extraordinary story', she said. 'Do you think she'd been drinking?'

'Drugs more likely if you want my opinion. Probably smoking pot. It would be in keeping with her image of herself.'

'But where had she been at that hour of the night?'

'My guess is that she'd been in Tim Moxon's apartment. Probably trying to seduce him.' After a pause she went on, 'The thing is, Rosa, do you think I ought to go and see how she is this morning? It would be the normal thing to do, but one's not dealing with a normal situation. She may now be perfectly all right. On the other hand she could still be nursing her malicious fantasies and I've no wish to be subjected to further abuse.' In a bleak tone she added, 'For all I know she's already told the police I attacked her.'

'I don't think you should approach her', Rosa said. 'If she's regained her senses, she'll probably get in touch with you to apologise. But if she hasn't, it's as well to keep out of her way.'

'Supposing she's died in the night?'

'I should think that's most unlikely, but if she has, let somebody else find the body!' She paused for a moment. 'I'm in court this morning, but would you like me to come down as soon as I'm free? I could be with you by mid-afternoon.'

'I'd welcome your support more than I can say, Rosa. I have a feeling that what happened last night was a sort of smokescreen to cover something more serious.' With a slight rasp in her voice, she added, 'I hope I'm not developing an imagination akin to Alison's. Anyway it'll be a relief to see you and I'll await your arrival with impatience.'

It was shortly after three o'clock that afternoon when Rosa turned into the drive of Deepwood Grange. The ramparts of leaves which had lined the way on her first visit had gone, removed by the contractor employed by the managing agents.

As the house came into view with its backdrop of trees on the rising ground behind, she noticed a number of cars parked in front. Amongst them was Doug Potter's Rolls Royce. She wondered if the police were back again. She left her car next to a florist's van and approached the house. She hoped the van didn't denote a delivery of wreaths.

As she reached the front door it opened and John and Desmond came out.

'Hello Rosa', Desmond exclaimed. 'What's brought you down again?'

'I had a free afternoon and thought I'd come and visit my godmother.'

'We've not seen her today', John remarked. 'She's all right, is she?'

It was apparent that Margaret's nocturnal encounter with Alison had not yet become generally known.

'Yes, she's fine', Rosa said. 'How are things here? Are the police still about?'

'They come and go', John replied. 'Des and I have been out quite a bit so we're not always up to date with what's going on.'

'Don't tell me that Alison doesn't keep you informed!'

'Haven't seen her today either', Desmond observed. 'I think she has a deadline for her book and has less time to surface in the real world.'

'I understand you had a lively meeting of the residents' association the other evening', Rosa remarked with a smile.

'It was more than lively', Desmond said with a laugh. 'Doug Potter charged around like a bull in a china shop and I felt almost sorry for Sir Wesley, who obviously wished he could send him down for life. As it was, the meeting broke up in confusion and smouldering dislike. All we agreed upon was to send flowers to David Anderson's funeral.'

'And that's been left to Alison to arrange', John chimed in, 'so he'll be lucky if they arrive.'

'Not that I expect he'll mind very much either way', Desmond said with a grin.

'If you'll excuse us, Rosa, we have to meet somebody', John now said briskly. 'Perhaps we'll see you later. Are you stopping the night?'

'I'm not sure. I've got a busy day tomorrow, so I'll probably go back tonight.'

'Anyway, hope to see you again soon', Desmond said as he turned to follow his friend.

The Great Hall was deserted and Rosa made her way over to the staircase leading to the balcony.

Margaret gave her a look of surprise as she opened the door and saw Rosa standing there.

'How did you get in?' she asked, almost accusingly.

'John and Desmond were coming out as I arrived.'

'Oh! I've not seen anyone today. A cup of tea or coffee?'

'Tea, please.'

Rosa followed her godmother into the kitchen.

'Any further developments?' she enquired. 'Incidentally, it was clear that John and Desmond knew nothing of what happened last night.'

'I'm not sure whether there've been further developments or not', Margaret replied mysteriously.

Rosa waited for her to go on, but she remained silent, staring at the kettle as though hypnotised by its inner murmuring.

'What about Alison?' Rosa asked. 'Have you spoken to her since last night?'

Margaret shook her head. 'I took your advice and haven't got in touch with her. And she's not been in touch with me either. But I have every reason to think she's been up to her mischief-making.'

'In what way?'

'I had a call from someone at Glass, Merrifield asking if I'd seen Tim Moxon or knew where he was. I said I'd not seen him and wasn't even aware that he was down here. I wasn't going to tell the person I'd seen his lights on in the small hours of the morning. The person on the phone then said they'd been expecting to hear from him first thing this morning, but hadn't. And, moreover, he wasn't answering his phone—'

'—Why were they calling you?' Rosa broke in.

'Exactly! That's what I wanted to know, and the person said he'd already spoken to Miss Tremlett, who had suggested that he should ring me as I might know something of Tim's movements. I told him I didn't and that I couldn't conceive why Miss Tremlett had suggested I might. He then apologised for bothering me and rang off.'

'I see what you mean about Alison mischief-making. I wonder why the person called her in the first place?'

'She's such a busybody, she's probably always on the phone to them about one thing or another and they've come to know her better than anyone else here.'

'What was the name of the person who called you?'

'It was Jeremy something or other. Quite an ordinary name. Yes, I remember, it was Jeremy Slater.' She paused. 'There's a bit more to the story. About an hour ago, I slipped out the back way and went across to Tim's apartment. His car was parked at the side where he always leaves it and I could see the curtains were still drawn across the windows. I went up the staircase that leads to his front door – it runs up the outside at the far end of the old coach house – and rang his bell. There was no answer. I then peered through the letter-box, but couldn't detect any sign of life inside.' She paused and gave Rosa a significant look. 'So what do you think we ought to do?'

The 'we' was not lost on Rosa and she was thoughtful for a while.

'I suggest we wait until it's fully dark, then see whether he has any lights showing and whether his car's still there.'

The truth was that Rosa was stuck for a more constructive suggestion.

'And supposing the answers to those questions are respectively no and yes, what then?'

'Let's just wait and see. In the meantime it might be an idea for me to go down and visit Alison. She'll obviously guess that you've told me what's happened, so I'll simply say that you're most upset by her allegations and I've come to find out how she is today. I'll obviously have to play it by ear, but a visit may help to answer a few questions.'

'And raise a few more', Margaret remarked in a mordant tone.

'Possibly', Rosa agreed.

Twenty minutes later Rosa rang the bell of Alison Tremlett's apartment. After a short delay the door was opened by a bleary-eyed Alison. She blinked stupidly at Rosa for a few moments.

'You woke me up', she said. 'I'd been trying to write, but my mind's not on work today. I suppose Margaret's told you everything?'

'She's very upset over what happened last night.'

'Has she admitted that she attacked me?'

'I'm sure you're confused about that, Alison.'

'You'd better come in', Alison said a trifle fretfully. 'We can't go on talking at the door.'

Rosa stepped inside and Alison closed the door and led the way into her sitting room.

'I'm not confused about anything. Margaret assaulted me and knocked me out with a blow on my head.'

'I accept that somebody knocked you out, but it couldn't have been Margaret.'

'Why not?' Alison asked in a querulous tone.

'Because she's not the sort of person who goes around doing that sort of thing and she certainly had no reason to attack you.'

'How do you know? You'd not seen her since you were a child until the other day. For all you know, she could have become a homicidal maniac.'

'Now you're being utterly fanciful', Rosa expostulated. But determined not to become ruffled, she quickly went on, 'How is your head today? Have you seen a doctor?'

'Not yet.' Her tone was curiously defensive.

'And you haven't reported the incident?'

'I'll probably mention it to Detective Chief Inspector James next time I see him.' She gave Rosa a sly look. 'Isn't it my public duty to report it? I mean, supposing she attacks others? Perhaps she already has.'

'If you're insinuating that Margaret had something to do with David Anderson's death, that's absurd.'

'That would be for the police to determine.'

'But Margaret had no motive to do any of the things you suggest', Rosa said with a note of exasperation.

'She's always disliked me and has never bothered to conceal it. She frequently snubs me in front of other people and I know she regards my books as trash. Don't deny it, Rosa, because it's the truth. I'm sorry to have to say it, but your godmother's a prig.'

'You're exaggerating, Alison. You've lost your sense of perspective.'

Alison suddenly swung round and looked Rosa straight in the face.

'Ask yourself, Rosa, how well do you really know Margaret? The answer is hardly at all. You tell me I'm exaggerating and being fanciful. You're just being blindly loyal.'

Rosa felt as if she'd received a stinging slap. It was true she had only recently renewed acquaintance with her godmother, but she still couldn't believe Alison's accusation. Couldn't or wouldn't, she wondered ruefully. She very much wished that Alison hadn't said what she had.

'Well, as long as you're all right', she said weakly, 'I'd better go back up to Margaret.'

'I can see I've given you cause for thought', Alison remarked complacently as she accompanied Rosa to the door.

It was a comment that immediately riled Rosa so that she became determined to regain the initiative.

'By the way, do you happen to know if Tim Moxon is down here?'

'Why do you ask me that?' Alison's tone was sharply aggressive.

'Only because Margaret thought she'd seen lights on in his apartment last night, but hadn't seen him about today. Somebody from his office apparently phoned to ask if she knew his whereabouts.'

'I've no idea where he is', Alison retorted in a calculatedly offhand tone.

'I gather his car is parked in its usual place.'

Alison blinked behind her spectacles which were the size of saucers.

'It's no good staring at me, Rosa, I'm not Tim's

keeper.' She suddenly smiled as if an amusing thought had come into her head. 'Let's hope he's not up someone's chimney.'

'The woman's mad', Margaret declared, when Rosa reported on her visit to Alison. 'Dangerously mad', she added for good measure. She went over to the window and looked in the direction of the coach house. 'There are still no lights in Tim's apartment. What do you think we ought to do?'

'I'll go and see if his car's still there', Rosa said.

'I don't advise using the back way. There's an unlit stone passage which is all right if you know it, but not otherwise. In any event there's no reason why you should make a furtive approach.'

'I'll be back in a few minutes', Rosa said, as she put on her coat.

'Perhaps I ought to come with you', Margaret said doubtfully.

'No, you stay here.'

Lights had been switched on in the Great Hall, but there was nobody about. When she got outside she noticed that most of the cars had gone, including Doug Potter's Rolls. Her own small Honda stood alone on the gravel forecourt. It was nearly half past five, though dark enough to be midnight.

She set off round the side of the building in the direction of the old coach house. As she turned the corner at the farther end of that building she almost bumped into Tim Moxon's car. It had clearly not been moved since Margaret had come reconnoitring earlier in the afternoon. Nevertheless she decided to mount the stairs leading to his apartment and satisfy herself there was nobody there. A peep through the letter-box revealed a totally dark interior, but from the waft of warm air in her face she deduced that the central heating was full on.

Obviously Tim didn't have to worry about fuel bills.

She was about to descend when a car's lights suddenly illuminated the bottom of the staircase. A moment later the engine was switched off and the lights extinguished. Somebody got out, closing the driver's door with no more than a muffled click.

Rosa held her breath. She was trapped at the top of a private staircase, with discovery only a few embarrassing seconds away. Bluff was her only chance.

'Is that you, Tim?' she called out boldly as a figure appeared at the bottom of the stairs. A man's head jerked back as he stared up at where she was standing.

'Who's that?' he asked, starting to ascend.

'I'm a friend of Tim's', Rosa said in a nervous gush. 'I've been ringing his bell, but can't get any reply.'

'He's presumably not in', the man said dispassionately.

'I don't think he can be.'

'We'll soon find out. I have a key.'

Rosa stared at him in surprise as he reached the small landing.

'May I ask your name?' he enquired politely. 'Incidentally, there is a light switch at each end of the staircase. I got the impression, however, that you preferred to remain in the dark.' The note of faint mockery in his voice was unmistakable.

'It's the first time I've been up here', Rosa said quickly. 'I didn't know where the switches were.'

'You've still not told me your name.'

She felt that refusal to reveal it was hardly an option open to her in the circumstances.

'I'm Rosa Epton. I'm visiting my godmother, Mrs Lakington, who lives in Apartment H.'

'Ah! Well, let's open the door and go in, shall we?'

'How fortunate that you have a key!'

'I'd better satisfy your curiosity, Miss Epton. It

happens to be my apartment. My name's Aldo Goran and I own Deepwood Grange.'

Turning his back on an embarrassed Rosa, he unlocked the front door and stepped inside, switching on a light as he did so. Rosa followed, observing the way he darted from room to room turning on further lights. It was as if he wished to make sure there were no bodies lying about.

'There's no sign of Tim, but I expect we could both do with a drink.'

He ushered Rosa into the living room, which was furnished like the showroom of a Park Lane penthouse. There was even a slender marble statuette of a shy young nymph standing on a lighted pedestal.

She noticed two unwashed glasses on a long, black onyx coffee table which stood in front of a white buckskin settee. There was also an ashtray full of butts. Aldo Goran wrinkled his nose in distaste as he followed Rosa's gaze and carried the offending items over to a small table by the door.

'Do you smoke, Miss Epton?' he asked as he joined her on the settee.

'No, I never have.'

'How sensible! Tim was obviously entertaining someone before he decided to disappear.' He turned to Rosa. 'Would you have any idea who it might have been?'

'None. I only came down this afternoon.'

'I'd prefer that he didn't smoke joints in my apartment', he said, giving Rosa a quizzical look. 'Personally I only smoke cigars. Havanas. Have you known Tim a long time?'

'No, only since I've been coming down here to visit my godmother.'

'He seems to get on well with the residents', Aldo Goran observed in a musing tone. 'Did you have any particular reason for visiting him now?'

Rosa took a deep breath. She realised that she was being gently interrogated, but felt there was nothing she could do about it.

'Mrs Lakington had been trying to phone him to ask him in for a drink, but couldn't get any reply, so I offered to come across. We thought his phone might be out of order.'

He nodded as he appeared to weigh her answer.

'How has Mrs Lakington reacted to the murder?' he enquired with disconcerting suddenness.

'She's very upset, like everyone else. The last thing any of the residents wanted was to become involved in a police investigation.'

'That's why I felt I must fly over. Tim Moxon has kept me in touch on the telephone, but I decided that wasn't enough. After all, Deepwood Grange is *mine*, even though the residents have purchased their apartments on long leases.'

'Did you ever meet David Anderson?' Rosa enquired.

He shook his head. 'I've never met any of the residents, though I sometimes feel I know them quite well. None of the apartments was sold without my personal approval, you see. You, I take it, Miss Epton, have met them?'

'Yes. There was a party the first time I came down and I was introduced to everyone then.'

'So you know Sir Wesley Binfield?'

'Yes.'

'A bit crusty, is he?'

'You could say that of a good many judges.'

'Of course, you're in the law yourself, are you not?'

'How do you know?'

'Tim Moxon must have told me.'

'What do you propose to do about Tim?' Rosa asked after a thoughtful pause. 'About his disappearance, I mean?'

'I'll make a few enquiries and if he hasn't turned up by tomorrow morning, I'll inform the police. Would that be a proper course, do you think?'

'It might be better to speak to Detective Chief Inspector James now and tell him that Tim is missing.'

'I'm glad to have your advice, Miss Epton. You know much more about these things than I do. I've got one or two calls to make and then I'll phone the police.' He leapt suddenly to his feet. 'I've never given you a drink', he exclaimed. 'What would you like?'

'Vodka and orange juice, if that's possible.'

'Of course it's possible. Do you prefer Russian or Polish vodka?'

'Polish, with freshly squeezed oranges from Florida.'

'Now you're mocking me.'

'It was my turn to do a bit of mocking.'

The telephone suddenly rang and he stared at it with an expression of annoyance, before reluctantly lifting the receiver.

'Yes, who is it?' he asked sharply. A moment later he handed the receiver to Rosa. 'It's Mrs Lakington', he said.

'Hello, Margaret, I'm in Tim's ... I mean Mr Goran's apartment. ... Yes, he's just arrived from Geneva. ... No, Tim's not here. ... Yes, I'm perfectly all right. ... I'll be back shortly.' She put down the receiver. 'That was my godmother fussing.'

'So I gathered.'

'I'd better drink up and go back.'

'I hope we shall meet again, Miss Epton. Incidentally, if Tim turns up, I'll tell him you've been trying to get in touch with him.'

There was no doubt in Rosa's mind that she was being gently mocked again.

CHAPTER 14

It wasn't long after Rosa had returned to Margaret's apartment that she received a call from Robin Snaith.

'That case of yours tomorrow morning, Rosa, is off', he said. 'I've just had a call from the officer in charge with the news that the chief prosecution witness has been involved in a car accident and been admitted to hospital, so there'll have to be an adjournment. He thought that if he could reach you, it would save you turning up at court. Fortunately I was still in the office. I gather your client's on bail, so there'll be no problem.'

'Thanks for letting me know, Robin.'

'Thank the officer. He's obviously a fan of yours.'

'I once saved his bacon for him and he's been embarrassingly grateful ever since.'

'How are things at Deepwood Grange?' Robin asked after a pause.

'I'll tell you when I see you.'

'Like that, is it? Well take care and remember you still have a partner to support.'

Rosa returned to the living room to find Margaret giving the television set some vigorous slaps.

'It's more effective than having the repair man come out here', she observed. 'And considerably cheaper.' When Rosa told her what the call had been about, Margaret immediately said, 'Then stay the night. I can easily find you a toothbrush.'

'I always carry one in the car, together with other spares', Rosa replied with a smile. 'I'll go down and fetch them.'

'Oh, I'm glad you'll stop. I still feel shaken by what happened last night and I'll be much happier if you're here.'

All the apartment doors were firmly closed and the Great Hall was deserted as Rosa made her way to the main front door. As she opened it, a man glanced round from the bell push panel which he was studying. A second later he let out an exclamation.

'It's Rosa Epton, isn't it?'

Rosa stared in surprise at the round, smiling face turned toward her. Though it was familiar, she was unable to place it. Her only thought was that it must be someone she had met in what she always referred to as her Chinese Case. Her client, who was charged with GBH, had been a waiter in a Chinese restaurant and used to turn up at court with a large entourage of brothers and cousins, who were apt to surround Rosa and talk to her all at the same time.

'I'm Peter Chen', the man now said, sending Rosa's thoughts swerving away on a completely different tack. 'We met in that diamonds case. I had a watching brief at the magistrates' court and was able to admire the way you demolished the prosecution's case and got your client off.'

Rosa blushed, partly at the compliment, partly at the closeness she had come to dropping an outsize brick.

'Of course I remember you', she said. 'As to my client on that occasion, it's always easier to get them off when the evidence falls apart of its own accord.'

His smile broadened. 'We both know that's an over-simplification. Anyway what are you doing at Deepwood Grange? You're not concerned in the murder, are you?'

'You know about David Anderson?'

The smile vanished as he said, 'He was both a client and a friend. Unhappily I've been abroad and have only just returned to England and heard what happened. Where do you fit in?'

'My godmother lives here and I visit her from time to time. I met David Anderson shortly before his death when I was here for the weekend.'

'Is there somewhere we can go and talk in private?' he asked in a suddenly urgent tone.

'Do you have a key to David's apartment? The police must have finished with it by now.'

'I don't think I ought to go in without their permission', he said doubtfully. 'Why don't we go somewhere for a drink? Somewhere right away from here.'

It was Rosa's turn to look doubtful. 'All right, but I must go and tell my godmother that I'm going out.'

'I passed a pub about a mile down the road. We can go there, have a couple of drinks and drive back.' He waved a hand in the direction of a gleaming BMW parked beside Rosa's small dirt-stained Honda. 'I'll wait for you in my car.'

On her way back inside, it struck Rosa as curious that Peter Chen had never said whose bell push he was looking for when she found him on the doorstep.

Margaret pursed her lips in slight disapproval when Rosa told her what had happened.

'You've done nothing but pop in and out since you arrived this afternoon', she remarked.

Rosa forebore to point out that most of the popping in and out had been on Margaret's account.

When she returned outside she could see Peter Chen sitting in the driving seat of his car. A subdued orange glow from the dashboard panel gave his face a more pronounced oriental appearance. He leaned over and opened the passenger door as she approached. Soft music filled the car and Rosa recognised the honeyed tones of Stevie Wonder, who happened to be one of her favourite singers. He started up the engine and the car took off like a rocket.

The car park at the Golden Goose public house was almost empty and a huge open fire of leaping flames greeted them inside. Peter Chen ushered Rosa to a corner seat close to the fire before going up to the counter and ordering. The publican was a cheerful, muscular, red-faced man who, despite a pronounced beer gut, still looked as if he could have pulled a farmer's cart uphill.

'Probably an ex-policeman', Chen commented when he returned with the drinks. 'Half the coppers in the country end up running pubs. Provides a very useful intelligence gathering service for the police in each area.' He raised his glass of orange juice. 'Here's to a fruitful collaboration.'

'Collaboration?' Rosa echoed in surprise.

'You and me', he said with a grin. 'If we pool our resources, we should be able to find out who killed David. It was obviously somebody at Deepwood Grange and it's therefore a mere process of elimination.'

'You make it sound very simple. Why are you so sure it must have been a resident?'

'Aren't you?'

'Yes, but I'd like to be fortified in my belief.'

'Ever since that diamond case David has been after the big boys who organised and carried out the heist. He'd spent months on the case, employed by the Dutch insurance company. His investigation led him to Deepwood Grange and he acquired an apartment there after he became certain he was on the right trail. He was fortunate in knowing Tim Moxon, which helped. He and Tim were neighbours in London.'

'That's a bit of a coincidence', Rosa observed with a slight frown.

Chen shrugged. 'Life's full of them.'

Rosa was well aware of the fact, but was still

suspicious when they cropped up in her cases. Especially if they were convenient coincidences.

'I'm sorry, I interrupted you', she said after a pause.

'He was obviously murdered because he'd become a threat to somebody and the somebody in question managed to strike first.'

'The choice of potential murderers at Deepwood Grange is limited', Rosa remarked drily. 'There are Doug Potter and Sir Wesley Binfield, both of whom are a bit long in the tooth for the role, or John Dixon and Desmond Murray who don't seem the type. You can rule out my godmother, Margaret Lakington, and also Alison Tremlett, neither of whom would have been physically capable of the crime. Mr and Mrs Unterby were abroad when it happened, so it couldn't have been them. Take your pick!'

'What about Tim Moxon?' Chen said.

'He's disappeared. At least, it looks that way.' Rosa then went on to relate what had happened since she'd arrived earlier that afternoon.

'I wonder what's happened to him', Chen said when she'd finished.

'There may be a perfectly innocent explanation, of course.'

'On the other hand he may be dead.'

'It depends on whether he was on the side of the angels.'

'He could be even closer to the angels now', Chen observed with a grim little smile.

Rosa glanced at her watch. 'I should be getting back. It's not fair of me to leave my godmother when I came down specially to hold her hand.' She paused. 'Incidentally, whose bell were you about to push when I found you on the doorstep?'

'Alison Tremlett's. David regarded her as a good source of information and I thought I'd start my

127

enquiries there. Also, I gather she had a crush on David.'

'She has crushes on anything in trousers younger than herself. David was the only good-looking bachelor within miles.'

'There was Tim Moxon.'

'Indeed, there was! I tend to overlook him as he isn't properly a resident. But he could certainly have been within her sights. Almost certainly was', she added, a second later, as she recalled Margaret's encounter with Alison in the small hours of the previous night. She had a feeling that whoever had knocked out Alison held the key to Tim Moxon's disappearance.

'And the two bachelors in Apartment A?' Chen said, breaking in on her thoughts. 'What about them?'

'They were immune to Alison's siren charms', Rosa said with a grin. 'She may have fantasised about them, but that would have been all. Her fantasies, of course, take over her books. You'd better watch out when you meet her.'

'I'm looking forward to that, particularly in view of what David once said about her.'

'What was that?'

'He suggested that the Alison Tremlett you all knew was a façade and that the real person lay well and truly hidden.'

'He didn't go as far as to suggest she was the brains behind the diamond robbery, did he?' Rosa enquired sardonically.

'He just described her as an enigma.'

Rosa was thoughtful as they left the pub and walked to the car.

'You know, I suppose, that Alison's apartment adjoins the unoccupied one in which David's body was found.'

Peter Chen nodded. 'If David had wanted to bug her apartment, he'd have found that very useful.'

CHAPTER 15

Charles and Janet Unterby were keep fit fanatics. Charles aimed to go for a five mile run each morning before breakfast and his wife often joined him and always did so at weekends. They reacted strongly to anyone referring to their exercise as jogging. The third member of their household who ran for sheer pleasure and not merely for the benefit of his mind or body was their Staffordshire bull terrier, Zonk. He was an engaging dog of immense strength and determination whose name said everything about him.

It was the Sunday following Rosa's brief visit to her godmother that Charles, Janet and Zonk set off around eight o'clock to pound their way through the surrounding fields and woods. In the three intervening days nothing further had happened. Tim Moxon was still missing and Aldo Goran had departed as unobtrusively as he had arrived. As Rosa suggested he had reported Tim's disappearance and then returned to London.

'Let's go through Flint Wood', Charles said when they had run about three miles. 'We haven't been that way for some time.'

Conserving her breath, Janet merely nodded. Zonk was meanwhile having a deliriously happy time chasing rabbits in a field off to their left. Charles called to him as they headed toward the wood and the dog came up like an express train just as they joined the track which entered it. Though he was apt to pant harder than his master or mistress, there was never any doubt who could keep going the longest.

It was about ten minutes later that Janet paused and called to him. Normally he responded immediately, if sometimes reluctantly, but on this occasion there was no sign of him.

Her husband then gave the whistle that was Zonk's particular call sign, while they stood on the grassy track and waited. But still he didn't come.

'He's obviously found something unusually interesting', Charles said between whistles.

'I hope nothing's happened to him', Janet remarked. 'We did once see an adder up here. Do you think he could have been bitten?'

'Not in November! However, I suppose we'd better go back just in case he's in trouble.'

They had retraced their steps about three hundred yards when Janet heard sounds coming from the undergrowth to their right. She indicated the direction.

'There's definitely something going on in those bushes', Charles agreed after listening for several seconds. 'I'll go and have a look.'

'It is Zonk', Janet exclaimed. 'He's making whimpering sounds. He must be hurt.'

The two of them thrust their way between bushes that grew wild over the floor of the wood. As Zonk heard them, his whimpers turned to barks.

They found him crouching in a small clearing, peering worriedly at something that lay just beyond the end of his nose. Scattered earth and leaf mould indicated that he'd been digging, as did the considerable amount of mud adhering to his face.

Charles, who was slightly ahead of his wife, came to an abrupt halt.

'Oh my God!' he said. Then: 'Don't come any nearer.'

A puzzled and excited Zonk was prodding at a plastic bag with his nose. It was possible to discern the features of a human head inside the bag. Tim Moxon's head.

CHAPTER 16

Fifty minutes later Charles Unterby was back at the shallow grave in which Tim Moxon had been buried. He was accompanied by Detective Chief Inspector James and other officers. Janet and Zonk were back in the apartment, with Zonk in a chastened mood of deprivation.

'Obviously your dog smelt something and began digging', James said matter-of-factly, as he stared down at the grisly sight. Apart from the head the body was entirely covered by loose earth and leaf mould. 'It looks as if the poor chap died the same way as David Anderson.'

'And presumably at the same hands', Charles remarked with an involuntary shiver.

'I never jump to conclusions in murder cases', James said austerely. He turned to one of the officers. 'Get back to the car, John, and radio the station. Say I want as many officers as can be mustered at this hour of a Sunday morning. The wood must be thoroughly searched and the public kept away until I say otherwise. Also, get a message to Phil that we have a nice job for a scenes of crime officer. And I don't want the body moved until the pathologist has seen it in situ.'

Detective Sergeant John Turner nodded briskly and, turning on his heel, departed like the messenger despatched from Aix to Ghent.

'Once Sergeant Turner gets back,' James went on, 'you and I can get down to the house, Mr Unterby.' Noticing that Charles was shivering, he added, 'I hope

131

you're not going to catch pneumonia for your pains.'

'I'm all right', Charles said, trying to control his shivering. 'I had a shower and a change of clothes between phoning and meeting you at the crossroads.'

'Good. *I* was about to dig into a plate of scrambled egg and bacon when the station phoned me. Sunday's the only day I eat breakfast. As it was I didn't even stop to kiss my wife goodbye. And my sons won't quickly forgive me. I'd promised to take them fishing today.'

He shook himself as if to dispel thoughts of a Sunday that might have been. 'Of course, you and Mrs Unterby were away at the time of the first murder, weren't you?'

'Yes. We were in Morocco.'

'Nice country?'

'We've been there before and like it. There's a reasonable guarantee of sunshine and not too many tourists at this time of year.'

'But still a lot of Arabs, I suppose!'

'You don't like them?'

'I'm not too fond of the ones I meet over here.'

'They're the millionaires.'

'I know. I have a prejudice against the species, probably because no policeman has ever become one.'

At that moment Detective Sergeant Turner returned to say that reinforcements were on their way.

'OK, John', DCI James said. 'Organise a good search and stay around until the pathologist comes.'

'I managed to catch someone from the photographic section, sir, and he should be here shortly. He was just leaving home for a game of golf. He didn't seem very pleased.'

James nodded sympathetically. 'There's nothing like the discovery of a body on a Sunday morning to disrupt life. It ought to be forbidden.' He turned to Charles. 'Ready, Mr Unterby?'

It was soon after the Unterbys had returned from their

run and Charles had set off to meet the police that Janet received a call from Alison Tremlett. Though it purported to be for nothing more than an innocent Sunday morning chat, Janet was sure that something had alerted Alison to phone at that particular moment. She had most probably seen them return from their run and observed their expressions. Then she would have noticed Charles leaving again in a hurry soon afterwards.

In the circumstances it was only natural that Janet should tell her of their gruesome discovery, which meant that it was not long before word had spread through the building.

Accordingly, by the time Chief Inspector James and Charles Unterby arrived at the house, the residents were gathered in small knots round the Great Hall, looking grim-faced and anxious.

Sir Wesley, who had been endeavouring to stay aloof from the others, immediately stepped forward.

'Ah, Chief Inspector, I've been waiting for you.' He glanced around him with disapproval. 'We've heard the news about Mr Moxon. Perhaps you'd like to come up to my apartment where we can talk more privately?'

'Yes', Alison chimed in. 'Sir Wesley and I are officers of the residents' association, you know.'

Sir Wesley glowered. 'I scarcely think this has anything to do with the residents' association as such', he said in a withering tone.

CI James held up a hand to still further argument. 'How many of you ladies and gentlemen have any information which might be useful to me in investigating Mr Moxon's death? In particular, which of you was the last person to see him alive?'

'I think I may be able to help you over that', Margaret Lakington said.

'I also have information on that point', Alison broke in excitedly.

'Thelma and I didn't even know he was down here', Doug Potter said. 'More to the point, what was Mr Goran doing here and why's he gone before we could talk to him?'

'It was Mr Goran who reported Mr Moxon's disappearance', James said. 'Apart from taking note, however, there was nothing we could do about it then, as there was no suggestion of foul play.' He glanced toward John Dixon and Desmond Murray. 'Do either of you know anything? When did you last see Mr Moxon?'

'As a matter of fact we saw him on Wednesday evening', John said. 'It was around eight o'clock. We'd just got back from Chichester. As we were putting the car away, Tim arrived and parked over by the coach house where he always left his car. He said he'd just come down from London, but wouldn't be here long.'

'Did he mention whether he'd be staying overnight?'

'He didn't say', Desmond replied. 'He struck us as being a bit on edge.'

'Worried? Anxious? Is that what you mean?'

'Yes. Not that he was ever really relaxed.'

'Did he say why he'd driven down?'

'Not exactly.'

'He either did or he didn't', James said quickly.

'He certainly didn't tell us why he was here, but we got the impression he was going to meet somebody.'

'What made you think that?'

'He kept on glancing at his watch and staring up at the windows of his apartment.'

'As if somebody might be up there waiting for him?'

'Yes.'

'Could you see whether there were any lights on in the apartment?'

'It appeared to be in total darkness', John said, while Desmond nodded.

'Did anyone see Mr Moxon after eight o'clock on

Wednesday evening?' James asked, glancing at the circle of now expressionless faces around him. Expressionless, that is, save for Alison Tremlett who seemed to be in the grip of some secret emotion. 'Do you wish to add something, Miss Tremlett?'

'Not here', she said, with a theatrical shudder.

'Of course. I understand. It's been helpful to me to address you together like this, but if perhaps you'd now return to your various apartments I can visit you individually in the course of the next couple of hours. Does that suit everyone?'

'My wife and I always attend morning service', Sir Wesley said stiffly. 'We'll be back at lunchtime should you wish to see me.'

'I'd still like to know what Mr Goran was up to, coming and going like that', Doug Potter broke in aggressively.

'I agree it's rather odd', Margaret said.

'I call it more than odd. For my money he's the bloke you want to get after, Chief Inspector. I bet he can tell you something about Moxon's death.'

'Thank you for the suggestion', James said drily. 'I'll bear it in mind.'

It was about an hour later that he rang the bell of Margaret's apartment and asked if he could come in.

'It won't be long before every apartment here is up for sale', Margaret said gloomily, as she led the way into the living room. 'And I can't see a rush of buyers after what's happened.'

CI James made no comment, but came straight to the point.

'I've just been talking to Miss Tremlett and she alleges that you assaulted her in the Great Hall four nights ago. Indeed, that you knocked her unconscious. I suppose I ought strictly to caution you before you make any reply—'

135

'—Caution or no caution, it's utter rubbish. The woman's out of her mind. Either that or she's brimming over with pure malice.'

'You're not surprised by her allegation?'

'Only because she made it to my face at the time and repeated it to my god-daughter, Miss Epton, the next day. If it's true, why didn't she report it immediately?'

'I naturally asked her that.'

'And?'

'She said she'd been unable to decide how seriously to take the matter, but with the discovery of Mr Moxon's body, she felt it her duty to tell the police everything.'

'I hope that included what she was doing there at three o'clock in the morning.'

'She told me she'd been unable to sleep and had gone outside for some fresh air.'

'In her negligée on a November night?' Margaret enquired scornfully.

'Instead of asking me questions, Mrs Lakington, it'd be better if you gave me your version of events.'

'Certainly, I will', Margaret said, and proceeded to do so.

'You're sure there were lights on in Mr Moxon's apartment when you looked out?' James said, when she had finished her recital of events.

'Quite sure.'

'And that would have been near enough two thirty on Thursday morning?'

'Yes.'

'How much time elapsed before you went downstairs to investigate the sounds you'd heard?'

'Not more than five or six minutes, I'd say.'

'They weren't loud noises?'

'No.'

'I'm surprised you could hear them at all in such a solidly built house', he said with a note of scepticism.

136

'After all, they had to reach you through at least two doors.'

'One door', Margaret said firmly.

'Your front door and your bedroom door.'

'I'd left my bedroom door open as the central heating had run wild and the room was far too hot.'

'The same heat that drove Miss Tremlett out for a breath of fresh air, would you think?' James enquired slyly.

'I know nothing about the temperature in her apartment', Margaret replied in her most imperious voice. 'I heard sounds and I went to investigate. I'm not given to prowling about in the small hours without good reason.'

'Nobody else seems to have heard anything.'

'Presumably because they were all asleep. I happened to be awake at the time. Anyway, what am I supposed to have struck Alison with?'

'I noticed a black ebony cane in the hall. . . .'

'I didn't take it downstairs when I went. Is that what she says I hit her with? Shall I fetch it for you to examine?'

'There's no hurry, Mrs Lakington. If it was the weapon, I'm sure it'll no longer bear any traces of having been used.'

'So at least if I'm a criminal, I'm an intelligent one!' Margaret observed scathingly.

James gave her a wintry smile. 'Is there anything else you'd like to tell me about the incident?'

'Yes. You said just now that Alison told you she'd gone out for a breath of fresh air and was attacked as she came back in.'

'Yes.'

'That's not what she told me', Margaret said with a small note of triumph.

'Go on then, Mrs Lakington.'

'She told me she'd been visiting a friend. Moreover, I've not the slightest doubt who the friend was. If you ask me, she'd been over in Tim Moxon's apartment.' She paused, trying to gauge CI James's reaction to what she'd just said, but his expression gave nothing away. She went on, 'I believe the law likes to assess issues on a balance of probabilities. Using that test, Chief Inspector, you have to admit that the scales come down heavily in my favour.'

But James was not in the mood to admit anything. He had learnt sufficient to know that villainy of the most vicious sort lurked at Deepwood Grange and he wasn't going to show his hand to any of its residents, whatever their airs and status.

Almost immediately he got up to leave and Margaret followed him out of the room.

'Am I still free to come and go at will?' she enquired with a note of sarcasm as they reached the front door.

'Certainly.'

'What's going to be done about Alison Tremlett's ridiculous accusation?'

'It'll be noted and considered, and in due course you'll doubtless learn what decision has been reached.'

'So I'm not being arrested here and now?'

He gazed dispassionately at her. 'You're not proposing to abscond, are you?'

'Of course not.'

'Then I've got nothing to worry about.'

Margaret hesitated. She knew she was behaving stupidly in a way, but she was worried.

'Does it depend on Miss Tremlett herself whether I'm charged?' she asked in a tight voice.

'It depends on a whole lot of things, Mrs Lakington.' He paused. 'I take it you accept that *somebody* attacked her?'

'She could easily have faked it', Margaret retorted,

and immediately wished she had not spoken so impetuously.

'Do you really believe that?' In a mildly chiding tone he added, 'On a balance of probabilities, that is?'

'All right, so somebody did assault her, but it was definitely not me.'

'I wonder who it was, then? Who else was up and about at three o'clock that morning?' He made to go. 'And why?'

Without waiting for answers to his questions, he nodded a farewell and departed.

CHAPTER 17

It was near enough eight thirty when CI James got home that Sunday evening. He expected to find a disgruntled family and was in no mood to hear all the things that had gone wrong since he had left the house that morning. Not that Alice was given to complaining; indeed she had accepted the lot of a senior detective's wife with few serious grumbles. He still marvelled at this when he recalled that she was not only twelve years his junior, but had also accepted the role of stepmother to two growing boys. And now the four of them were looking forward to the arrival of an additional member of the family. Paul and Jonathan were both hoping for a brother, their father for a daughter and Alice for whatever turned up.

He came in to the living room to find his sons absorbed in a video of a World Cup soccer match and Alice, her feet up on the settee, browsing through a Sunday paper.

'Hi, Dad', Jonathan said, turning his head away from the TV screen for a couple of seconds. 'I've been down to the beach with Alan and his father. It was great. We dug in the sand for bodies.'

'Find many?' James enquired, as he went over and gave his wife a kiss.

'No, worse luck.'

'What have you done today, Paul?' he asked his elder son.

Paul let out a gasp and flung himself back in his chair as the West German goalkeeper made a spectacular save.

'I went round to Gavin's and helped him and his dad with the boat. Mrs Prince cooked a smashing dinner.'

Mr Prince's boat was a well-known local landmark. It was being built in their front garden and there were those who doubted if it would ever reach the sea. All helping hands were welcome in its construction.

'Hungry?' Alice said, as David James gazed with relief at the tops of his sons' heads. He felt he didn't deserve to find such harmony after abandonment of their fishing expedition.

'I think so', he replied with a weary sigh.

'It won't take me long to warm up your dinner. The boys and I have already fed as we weren't sure when you'd be back.'

'I'll come and lend a hand', he said as he followed her out to the kitchen. 'And what sort of a day have you had, darling?'

'Quiet. After Paul and Jonathan had gone out, I got on with a few overdue domestic chores. Then I phoned Camilla and suggested she come round for a snack, which she did.' She gave her husband a grin. 'I supplied the food and she brought all the gossip from the theatre. Who's going to be in what next season; and who's on the way up and who's on the way down.'

'By which you mean, who's in whose bed', her husband remarked.

'There was a certain amount of that, too. Anyway,

that was my day, what about yours?' she asked, putting her arms round his neck and kissing him warmly. 'Is the case any nearer to a solution?'

He held her close to him in silence before replying.

'I think so', he said at length. 'There are still some pieces missing, but I believe I'm closing in. There's only one snag. There's no evidence.'

And that was near enough the truth. It had been a long day in which he and others had worked flat out in the search for clues. The pathologist had confirmed that Tim Moxon had died the same death as David Anderson. That he had most probably been rendered unconscious by a squirt of gas (nitrous oxide seemed most likely) before having the plastic bag put over his head and sealed tightly round his neck with adhesive tape. His hands had been secured behind his back with a length of common flex which could have come from anywhere.

A search of Moxon's apartment at Deepwood Grange had revealed nothing of significance, any more than had a search of the area where his body was found. His murderer belonged to the professional class.

The body had obviously been conveyed to within fifty yards of its burial place by car, but nobody appeared to have seen or heard anything, despite enquiries at farms and cottages in the area. His nocturnal funeral had gone unwitnessed.

With varying degrees of acquiescence the residents of Deepwood Grange had consented to an examination of their respective cars. Sir Wesley Binfield had been the most put out by the request, though James had attributed this to an inflated sense of dignity, rather than a guilty conscience. At all events, the examination of each of their cars had produced nothing by way of evidence. None showed any sign of having borne Tim Moxon to his lonely resting place. If one had been so used, all evidential traces had been successfully removed.

Mud and small stones and other debris had been carefully collected from the wheels and interiors for further examination, but James was not overly hopeful.

Following his initial interview with Tim Moxon in London and as a result of what he had learnt from Peter Chen and Wanda Velasquez, he was in no doubt that David Anderson had been stalking a prey who had become suspicious and had struck first. Presumably, Anderson must have given himself away at some point. But where exactly did Tim Moxon's death fit in? If he had chosen to be more forthcoming with the police, he might still be alive. James suspected from his habitual demeanour that he had probably found himself caught in the middle and pulled in two directions. He had not had sufficient strength or courage to take what might have been the hard option.

From a practical point of view, his murder, and more particularly the subsequent disposal of his body in the wood, must have required at least two people. By the same token, it was most unlikely that one person could have managed to kill David Anderson and put his body up the chimney.

If that were so, it ruled out Mrs Lakington and Miss Tremlett. Neither would have had the physical ability, though the two crimes might well belong to Alison Tremlett's world of fantasy.

That left the Binfields, the Potters, the Unterbys and the two young men in Apartment A. The Unterbys had been away when Anderson was killed and it was scarcely likely that they would have gone through the charade of finding Moxon's body if they'd taken the trouble to bury it in the first place. James felt that Zonk would clear them if he were able to tell his own story.

As for the Potters and the Binfields, it was stretching the imagination to see either murder as the work of a husband and wife team. That left John Dixon and

Desmond Murray. They alone were physically capable of the two crimes. But they had been polite and co-operative and appeared to have nothing to hide. Moreover, neither had a criminal record of any sort. They weren't even on any unofficial record as being known homosexuals, which was a measure of their discreetness.

As a matter of course he had checked each of the residents with the Criminal Record Office and had been interested to discover that Alison Tremlett had a conviction under the Fraudulent Mediums Act of 1951 for which she had been fined fifty pounds; also one for impersonating a police officer for which the fine had been one hundred pounds. In the first case, she had organised a séance at which a plate had been passed round for alms. This resulted in a complaint by one of those attending that she had been threatened with disagreeable consequences at the hands of the spirits if she refused to give anything. In the second case it appeared that Alison had pretended to be a woman detective officer in order to bring pressure on a recalcitrant husband to keep up maintenance payments to his separated wife, who had become a friend of hers.

Both offences confirmed the world of fantasy she moved in, but still didn't make her a probable murderer.

The only other resident with any criminal convictions was Doug Potter. He had two convictions for GBH while still in his twenties for which he had been sent to prison. And shortly before World War II he had served four years for burglary. He had then been thirty-two. Thereafter he had either turned over a new leaf or contrived not to be caught. After the war he had made a quick fortune dealing in army surplus and generally wheeling and dealing in black market transactions – the sort where the purchaser asked no questions and the seller accepted only cash. Nevertheless it seemed that

Doug Potter had stayed out of the law's clutches for over forty years. He was now seventy-six, but as tough as they came. Was it possible that he was still involved in crime? Crime of a more sophisticated and deadly nature?

Sir Wesley had eventually told James about the case in which a young Binfield had defended a young Potter on a murder charge. He had been eager to learn what else the police knew about Potter, but James had not satisfied his curiosity. In view of his convictions for grievous bodily harm, an acquittal for murder didn't stand out as starkly as it might otherwise have done, even though Sir Wesley had been at pains to stress that the verdict didn't reflect the true facts.

But if Doug Potter had resorted to murder again, he must have had an accomplice. Who could it have been?

It was at this point his wife steered him to the kitchen table and a plate of steak and kidney pie, with feathery mashed potato and cauliflower in a cheese sauce.

'If it tastes as good as it looks and smells,' he said, 'I'm the luckiest officer in the county. Fancy having a wife who's as pretty as a dream and cooks like one.' She stood at his side as he sat down and he rested his head against her stomach. 'How's Liza today?'

'Very quiet. Obviously knows it's Sunday. Incidentally, Jonathan met a girl called Fiona when he was out today and thinks that's much nicer name, though he's still going to pray for a brother.'

'Well, he's going to have a sister and her name's going to be Liza', James said firmly, as he took a mouthful of food and let out a contented sigh.

Left on his own for a few minutes while Alice went upstairs, he fell once more to thinking about events at Deepwood Grange. Although the method of execution had been identical in both cases, he was unsure how far they were related. Certainly motive seemed to be different.

144

He recalled somewhat ruefully having said after the discovery of David Anderson's body that if he knew the motive, he would know who committed the crime. But it wasn't proving as easy as that.

The murderer was, so to speak, centre stage, but remained frustratingly faceless.

A vital clue was missing and he wished he knew what to look for.

CHAPTER 18

Rosa had risen late that Sunday morning. She had been to the theatre the previous evening and then out to dinner. Her companion had been a rugger-playing young barrister who had clearly taken rather a shine to her. She had known him for several months and they had been out together a number of times. She had found him quite amusing at first, but was now of the view that the only topic of conversation which really interested him was himself. She was tired of hearing of his exploits in court and on the rugger field and coming on top of an extremely tedious play (his choice), she knew she had had enough of him. She couldn't think how she had ever been fooled by his earnest friendliness. He was just a bore.

Rosa not infrequently despaired of her so-called love life, though not as often as her friends did. The young men who were trotted out for her approval usually left her cold and the few short-lived affairs she had had were always with impudently amoral young men who would make hopeless husbands and fathers, whatever their attractions in bed. Even so, she regarded herself as more

fulfilled than a lot of her married girl-friends who took it
upon themselves to despair on her behalf.

Her Sunday morning thoughts on the subject came to
an abrupt end when the phone rang and she heard
Margaret's agitated voice on the line.

'They've found Tim Moxon's body and I've just had
that chief inspector here.'

It was several minutes before Rosa had a chance of
interjecting anything other than a sound to indicate she
was still listening.

'I'm not easily upset, as I think you know', Margaret
went on, 'but how much more can I put up with?' She
paused and then said in a taut voice, 'Do you think I'll be
charged with assaulting Alison, preposterous though
that would be?'

'I doubt it very much', Rosa said. 'In any event the
police are unlikely to take any action until they've
cleared up their main enquiry. That will be time enough
for them to decide what to do about peripheral issues.'

'I don't find that particularly comforting', Margaret
remarked bleakly. 'The very fact I'm in any danger at all
of being prosecuted on the word of a crazy female
undermines one's confidence in British justice. I never
believed that sort of thing could happen.'

It could happen, Rosa reflected, because there was no
such thing as absolute justice, as so many people
innocently imagined. It was a concept influenced this
way and that by the imperfections, and sometimes the
downright wickedness, of human nature. Rosa had
always regarded justice as one of the most emotive of
words, but this was not the moment to tell her
godmother.

'When will you be able to come down again?'
Margaret now asked hopefully.

'I'm in court tomorrow, but I'll call you in the
afternoon.' She paused. 'I do realise what an anxious

time you're having, but I assure you that you're not in any danger of imminent arrest.'

'Imminent arrest! Talk about cold comfort on the Sabbath!'

'I'm sorry, I didn't mean it like that at all. I was just trying to put things into a proper perspective. What's happened is ghastly and the discovery of Tim's body makes it even worse. I just hope the police can bring their enquiries to a quick conclusion. It's possible Tim's murder may assist them to do that, though it sounds cold-blooded to say so.'

Their conversation ended with Rosa trying, not too successfully, to summon up words of comfort and exhortation and promising to ring that evening.

News of Tim Moxon's murder had shocked her, but not come as a total surprise. His disappearance, though susceptible of an innocent explanation, had been ominous. Her immediate thoughts, however, were not on who had killed him, but on where Aldo Goran fitted in. His sudden appearance at Deepwood Grange just after Tim had vanished was more than curious in the circumstances, and Rosa couldn't help wondering if her unexpected encounter with him had impinged upon his plans. But what plans?

As she contemplated her recent conversation with Margaret she began to feel guilty. It was obvious her godmother would have liked her to go down that afternoon, and she had no real excuse for not doing so, save that she was tired and had been looking forward to a lazy Sunday at home. Even if she called back now and started off immediately, it would be dark within a couple of hours of her arrival and she didn't fancy a wet drive back along pitch-black roads. Though it wasn't actually raining at that moment, a look at the sky quickly persuaded her that it was about to start.

And even if she did drive down, what could she do

when she got there, apart from offering the same cold comfort that had been acidly dismissed? She was sure the police would not take any further action on Alison's outlandish accusation. Furthermore, that Alison herself would never start a private prosecution for assault. It might not be very comfortable for either of them to continue living under the same roof, but then the murders had done that for all the residents.

Rosa had a long, luxurious bath while she pondered all this. By the time she dried herself, she had squared her conscience about not going down. When, as promised, she called Margaret in the evening, she would suggest a visit the following weekend.

It was almost unbelievable that only a month had passed since Margaret's letter had arrived out of the blue at the office. Rosa wondered how their relationship might have developed in the absence of the gruesome events that had taken place. She reflected with a smile that Margaret would always be a forceful influence in anyone's life, even without any accompaniment of murder.

What had happened at Deepwood Grange was theatrically macabre. The curious assortment of residents, an owner who seemed as insubstantial as the Cheshire Cat in *Alice in Wonderland* and two horrific murders, which had in some way to be connected.

Putting on a pair of jeans and a sloppy sweater, Rosa went into the kitchen to make herself a cup of coffee. While it was brewing, she nibbled at a water biscuit. The meal they had had at a Greek restaurant the previous evening was still making itself felt.

She took her coffee and half-eaten biscuit into the living room and sat down on the settee, tucking her legs beneath her. Her mind went back to her very first visit to Deepwood Grange and to the party in the Great Hall where she had met everyone. She recalled her first sight of Tim Moxon as he emerged from the unoccupied apartment in which David Anderson's body was subsequently to be discovered. Tim wore the anxious expression she later came to associate with him and she remembered his making a beeline for Anderson, who was standing alone, glass in hand. Desmond Murray had intercepted him and introduced Rosa to him, but he had excused himself after a brief exchange of pleasantries. Later Desmond had introduced her to David Anderson, who had somehow looked out of place at the party.

She had taken to Desmond immediately. He had a friendly, engaging manner and she felt it was a waste that he was gay. He certainly didn't look it, but she had lived long enough to know that homosexuals didn't all have limp wrists and a giveaway walk. People who thought that, her partner, Robin, used to say, probably believed the Queen put on her crown every time she left the palace.

She remembered Desmond telling her that he and John had bought their apartment as an investment and that they never stayed anywhere very long. As things were going, nobody was likely to stay there very long. She frowned as she tried to recall something that had flitted across her mind in the café where she and Margaret had had Saturday morning coffee with the two boys. What had it been? It was no more than a momentary impression, which now lay buried in her subconscious and was unwilling to be dredged up.

She finished her coffee and left the half-eaten water biscuit in the saucer. She couldn't decide whether she wanted a Sunday paper sufficiently to walk down three flights of stairs and then back up again. On balance, she thought not. She might go for a walk in the course of the afternoon and buy one then.

She glanced across at her briefcase resting on its usual chair, almost as if it were a pet. The papers in Mickey

149

Rogers's case were inside and she must spend some time on them.

Mickey Rogers on a Monday morning was not a prospect that filled her with much joy. She hadn't heard from him for over a week and wondered if he had run to earth his vital witness, John Baraski. She thought it highly improbable. The police had obviously had an ulterior motive in allowing Mickey bail and she wondered if it had been fulfilled. She even wondered whether Mickey would answer to his bail the next day. It wouldn't surprise her at all to arrive at court and find he had gone over the side. Mondays always seemed to bring their own aggravation.

About an hour later she roused herself to go out. A brisk walk in the park would do her good, after which she could turn on the lights, draw the curtains and shut herself away for the rest of the day. Her tiny flat on Campden Hill was within a few minutes' walk of Notting Hill Gate, with Hyde Park not far to the east.

By the time she returned home it had begun to drizzle and it was with a cosy feeling that she shut out what was left of the day.

Around seven o'clock she called Margaret, but could get no reply. Rosa assumed she had gone for a drink with one of her neighbours and felt relieved that her godmother wasn't brooding alone at home. She would call later in the evening.

But at half past nine there was still no reply. Probably she had been persuaded to stay and have a meal with whomever she was visiting. Rosa knew that Sunday evenings were a favourite time for genteel socialising amongst the residents.

Even when the phone remained unanswered an hour later, Rosa wasn't really worried, though she did think that Margaret might have called her to say she was going out. But perhaps that wasn't practicable. At all events she went to bed without any undue sense of foreboding. She would ring her in the morning before she left for court.

But in the morning she was still unable to get any response. She sought the operator's help, only to be informed that there didn't appear to be any fault on the line.

CHAPTER 19

As she got ready to leave for court that Monday morning, Rosa pondered over her failure to get in touch with Margaret.

By now she was distinctly worried. At best, it seemed, her godmother must be lying stricken on the floor of her apartment, unable to raise help. At worst . . . but that didn't bear contemplation.

An obvious move was to call the Binfields or John and Desmond and ask them to go and investigate. But anxious as she was she shrank from striking such an alarmist note. There was already alarm enough at Deepwood Grange without her adding to it. And as for alerting the police, that would be even more extreme.

In the event she decided to go to court and hope that her case would be over by mid-morning. Then she would return to her office and make further efforts to get in touch with Margaret. Unless she received positive reassurance she would jump into the car and drive down immediately. She just prayed that her worst fears would be dispelled, without trying to articulate precisely what they were. She'd had one nightmarish moment when in her mind's eye she'd seen her godmother lying dead with a plastic bag tied over her head, but she had quickly dismissed this possibility as coming from an overheated imagination.

Half an hour later she parked her car in a side street near the court. Fulham Magistrates' Court was one of her chief stamping grounds and she got on well with its officials, including the two stipendiaries who shared duty there. The senior, Mr Dill, had been a stipendiary magistrate for so long that he had become encrusted with idiosyncrasies and, in appearance, was not unlike an ancient crustacea. He was due to retire the following Easter, a moment which his staff impatiently awaited. The junior magistrate was Ms Charlton, an out and out feminist whom the police not unnaturally regarded with considerable suspicion, but who, for all that, dispensed justice with brisk efficiency and complete confidence. She was married to a businessman about whom little was known, save that his name wasn't Charlton.

As Rosa turned a corner of the court, she at once saw Mickey Rogers. He was standing on the pavement outside the entrance, obviously on the look-out for her. As soon as he spotted her he came hurrying up.

''Ello, Miss Epton, I was worried you might 'ave got 'eld up or forgotten to come.'

The irony of his observation was not lost on Rosa, but she refrained from telling him what had passed through her own mind.

'I'm not late', she said defensively.

'It's just that I don't like courts. Too many people trying to do you down. But with you defending me I know I'll be all right.'

'Nothing dramatic's going to happen today. The prosecution will obviously ask for you to be committed for trial at the crown court and there's not much we can do to prevent that.'

'As long as you get me bail again, Miss Epton. I've got

to 'ave bail.'

'The police didn't oppose bail last time, so I don't see why they should on this occasion. After all,' she went on with a smile, 'you've turned up safely this morning. By the way, how is your girl-friend?'

'She worries about me. I keep telling 'er the baby'll be born with a ruddy great frown on its little face.'

'Have you spoken to Sergeant Grierson recently?'

''E phoned last night to make sure I'd be 'ere this morning. I told 'im if I'd been going to skip, I'd 'ave skipped. 'E sounded a bit funny to me, but 'e didn't say anything else.'

'What about your friend John Baraski? Any news of him?'

Mickey made a sour face. 'I reckon 'e's done a proper bunk. 'Im and the girl what nicked the ring. It really annoys me the way these foreign types come over 'ere and behave as if they owned the place.'

Rosa glanced at him with one eyebrow quizzically raised.

'No, I mean it, Miss Epton. They're just parasites. That's what they are, parasites.'

'Well, we'd better go inside, Mickey, before the police start shouting for you', Rosa said. She never ceased to marvel at some of the moral stances adopted by her clients.

As they entered the court portals Detective Sergeant Grierson stepped forward from a group of uniformed officers who were studying the list of cases pinned to a board on the wall. He looked in ill-humour, which might mean anything on a Monday morning; though Rosa knew he was cross at her refusal to accept a formal committal for trial on the statements and her insistence on the attendance of witnesses.

'You're late', he said to Mickey. 'I told you to be here at ten.'

'I was 'ere. I was talking to my solicitor outside, wasn't I, Miss Epton?'

'Go and report to the jailer now', Grierson said peremptorily. Turning to Rosa he went on in a tone almost as brusque, 'I'd like to have a word with you, Miss Epton. Let's go over to that corner.'

Rosa followed him across the lobby to a small alcove, wondering what was coming next. What did come was totally unexpected.

'I'm prepared to have the case dealt with summarily if your client will plead guilty', he said, watching her closely.

'Plead guilty here this morning, you mean?'

Sergeant Grierson nodded. 'It'll save everyone a lot of trouble.'

He's up to something, Rosa thought, her lawyer's natural suspicion aroused.

'Are you certain the magistrate would agree to summary trial?' she asked. 'After all, handling a stolen ring valued at eighty thousand pounds isn't normally a summary matter.'

'I'm sure we could persuade her between us', he said with a small, wintry smile.

'It's Audrey Charlton sitting, is it?'

'Yes. She can give him six months and everyone'll be satisfied.' He paused. 'It's a deal, is it?'

'I wouldn't think so for a moment', Rosa replied.

Sergeant Grierson frowned angrily. 'It's the best offer Mickey's every likely to get, but if you're not prepared to advise him to accept . . .' He gave an expressive shrug.

'Isn't the prosecution legally represented?' Rosa asked, slightly puzzled.

'There's been a hitch', Grierson said in an offhand tone. 'The Yard solicitor's rep can't manage the case today. But if Mickey pleads guilty, that doesn't matter. I can tell the court the facts. I've cleared it with my DI.'

'I see. Well, I'd better go and talk to Mickey, but don't expect too much.'

'If we can't deal with the case as I've suggested, I'll be opposing a continuation of bail', he said with a sly smile.

'Is that a threat?'

'I'm just telling you, so that you can pass it on to your client.'

'What grounds do you have for opposing further bail?' Rosa enquired in a dangerously quiet tone.

'Don't worry about that! There's never a shortage of grounds with somebody like Mickey Rogers.'

He turned on his heel and disappeared through the door leading to the jailer's office. Rosa stared after him with a thoughtful expression. After a moment she glanced about her. The entrance lobby was now crowded, mostly with witnesses waiting to give evidence in a variety of cases. There was nobody amongst them, however, who remotely resembled a wealthy Egyptian lady who wore eighty thousand pound rings. Moreover, if Mrs Osman had been there, surely Sergeant Grierson would have gone across to speak to her. Officers usually treated their witnesses like hens with newly hatched chicks.

So that was it! Mrs Osman was missing and without her evidence the prosecution had no case. Hence Sergeant Grierson's attempt to extract a plea of guilty, which would obviate the necessity of calling witnesses.

It was a devious trick and Rosa was determined to make him regret it.

She made her way into court and sat down in the lawyers' row. As she bowed to the bench, Audrey Charlton gave her a wisp of a smile.

Ms Charlton was a tiny woman with small, pointed features framed by black hair cut in a straight fringe. She invariably dressed in mixtures of black and white and wore huge, round spectacles which seemed to cover half her face.

As Rosa tuned in to the proceedings, it was to realise that the magistrate was having an altercation with a red-faced police inspector who had unwisely tried to put pressure on her in her own court and was now being firmly put in his own place.

It was another twenty minutes before Rosa's case was called on and Mickey Rogers took his place in the small, railed-off area that comprised the dock. As he did so, Sergeant Grierson stepped into the witness box.

'I ask for a further remand in this case, Your Worship', he said bluntly.

Ms Charlton frowned. 'I don't understand', she said in a steely voice. 'The court has specially set aside time to hear the case. Why isn't the prosecution ready to go ahead?'

'An unforeseen difficulty has arisen, Your Worship', Sergeant Grierson said stonily.

'I still don't understand.'

'As I explained, Your Worship, an unforeseen difficulty has arisen.'

'You've explained nothing, Officer. What difficulty are you referring to?'

'Mrs Osman, who is a vital witness, is unable to come to court today.'

'Has she sent a medical certificate to that effect?' Ms Charlton enquired coolly.

'No, Your Worship.'

'Why can't she be here?'

'She's had to go away.'

'When did you first discover that?'

'Only yesterday.'

The magistrate turned to Rosa. 'This seems very unsatisfactory, Miss Epton. The court sets aside time to hear the case, only to be told at the eleventh hour that it can't go on. Is there anything you'd like to add?'

'When I arrived at court this morning, Your Worship, Sergeant Grierson indicated to me that he would be prepared to accept a summary trial in certain circumstances. I would agree to that course, but should mention that the plea would be one of not guilty.'

Ms Charlton turned back to Sergeant Grierson who was scowling angrily.

'I can't proceed without my main witness', he said stubbornly. 'I must still ask for a remand.'

'Do you object to a further remand, Miss Epton?'

'I certainly do, Your Worship. The prosecution has had more than sufficient time to prepare its case and, if it's still not ready to proceed, I urge you to dismiss the charge here and now.' She glanced about her as if looking for someone in a crowd. 'It doesn't seem that the police have even sought legal representation.'

'That had occurred to me, too', the magistrate observed, turning back to Sergeant Grierson who was standing like a furious minor deity in the witness box. 'Have you not sought legal representation?'

'I will be represented at the next hearing, Your Worship', he said defiantly.

'Perhaps the court could be told where Mrs Osman has gone and how long she's expected to be away', Rosa interjected in a velvety tone.

'What's the answer to that?' Ms Charlton said.

'I'm unable to say where she's gone, Your Worship.'

'I take it that means he doesn't know', Rosa remarked.

'You've no idea where she's gone or when she'll be back, that's the truth, isn't it?' the magistrate said with asperity. 'What nationality is she?'

'Egyptian, Your Worship.'

'For all you know she may have left the country for good, isn't that the long and short of it?'

'I have no reason to believe that at all', Sergeant Grierson replied, resembling more than ever a climber clinging precariously to his last hold.

'Or to disbelieve it', Ms Charlton remarked dismissively, as she glanced down at the court register on the desk in front of her.

Even if the magistrate did grant a further remand, there would be no question of bail being refused.

'Well, Miss Epton?' she said, looking up.

'I submit that the police have been blatantly dishonest in their handling of this matter, Your Worship, and I ask you to dismiss the charge. It wouldn't be fair on my client to prolong his ordeal. Moreover, it's only right I should tell Your Worship that Mr Rogers has a complete answer to the charge. His possession of the ring in question was wholly innocent and it's more than a pity that the police acted so precipitately in arresting him.'

'Thank you, Miss Epton', the magistrate said and went on, 'It seems to me that the court has been treated with scant respect by Sergeant Grierson in this matter. I do not consider that the application for a further remand is justified and I, accordingly, dismiss the charge.' She glanced across at Mickey Rogers who had been following the exchanges with the lively interest of a spectator at a Wimbledon final. 'You are free to leave the court', she announced.

A few moments later as Rosa was pushing her way out of court, a voice spoke softly in her ear.

'You've done it again, Miss Epton.'

She turned to see the smiling face of Peter Chen just behind her.

'What on earth are you doing here?' she said in utter surprise.

'I wanted to hear what happened in your case.'

'What's your interest in Mrs Osman's ring?' Rosa enquired sardonically.

'Put like that, none.'

'And, anyway, how did you know the case was on today?'

'Ask the right questions of the right people and you can usually find out anything', he replied with a grin. 'You really twisted that officer's tail, it was a delight to hear.'

'I had the magistrate on my side.'

'I agree that helped.'

'You've heard what's happened to Tim Moxon?'

Peter Chen nodded gravely. 'I was down at Deepwood Grange yesterday.'

Rosa's eyes opened in further surprise.

'What time did you leave?'

'I stayed longer than I'd intended. I started back around ten o'clock.'

Rosa wondered what had been the reason for his visit, but didn't like to ask so forthright a question. But she could at least enquire whether he had seen her godmother.

'No, Alison was the only person I saw', he said in answer to her question. 'The place was dead when I arrived in mid-afternoon and I imagine they were all still having their siestas.'

'And how was Alison?' It wasn't that Rosa particularly wanted to know, but she hoped to learn more about his visit.

'She was very upset over Tim's death. She's sure further terrible things are going to happen and that her own life is in danger.'

Rosa made a scornful sound. 'I suppose she told you of my godmother's alleged assault on her?'

'As a matter of fact, she now thinks Mrs Lakington is behind everything that's happened there.'

'She's insane', Rosa said in a resigned tone.

'She believes your godmother is mixed up in some

159

diamond smuggling racket', Chen went on. 'I gather Mrs Lakington lived in South Africa and was married to someone in the diamond business.'

'That doesn't make her a criminal', Rosa said indignantly.

'I'm merely telling you what Alison said, as I gathered you were interested in my visit', Chen said mildly. Glancing past Rosa, he went on, 'I think your client wants to speak to you. I'll wait for you outside the court.'

As he left her side, Mickey Rogers approached.

'I've gotta get back to my girl,' he said, 'but I couldn't go without thanking you. You were terrific. As for Sergeant Grierson, I 'ope 'e catches a cold up 'is backside, if you'll excuse my sentiments.'

'You'd better steer well clear of him', Rosa said. 'Also, don't go minding diamond rings for any more of your friends.'

'Don't worry, I've learnt my lesson.'

And how often have I heard that before, Rosa reflected.

'You remember asking me about that diamond smuggling job last time we met?' Mickey went on. 'Are you still interested?'

'Why, have you found out something further?' Rosa asked, suddenly curious.

Mickey grinned at her. 'Listen to this for a giggle. . . .'

But Rosa didn't giggle. Instead she felt as if a bucket of icy water had been hurled in her face.

She turned and hurried out of the building, scarcely aware of Peter Chen falling into step beside her. He glanced at her enquiringly, as she began to run.

'I have to get back and phone Deepwood Grange', she said in a tone of great urgency.

CHAPTER 20

Aldo Goran had always prided himself on his judgement and sense of timing. To be successful one had to know when to move in and, more particularly, when to move out.

His visit to Deepwood Grange, coinciding as it did with Tim Moxon's disappearance, had been a first move toward what had become an inevitable end. He was a fatalist and clearly foresaw it.

What had still been uncertain at that time had been when Tim's body would be discovered. Thanks to Zonk it had been sooner rather than later, but Aldo Goran bore the dog no ill will.

In fact he felt rather more irked by Rosa than by Zonk. Their unexpected meeting outside the coach house apartment had been most tiresome, though he was pleased to think he had handled their encounter with aplomb. But it would have been better still if it had never taken place.

He had returned to London in the early hours of the next morning and flown back to Geneva that same day.

He had subsequently learned of the discovery of the body within hours of the event and had realised that the end couldn't be long delayed.

It was David Anderson's arrival at Deepwood Grange that had put a fly in the ointment and that was entirely down to Tim Moxon. It was Tim who had recommended Anderson as a suitable resident and who had thereby shown himself to be a traitor. He must have known what

Anderson was up to and now he had paid the price for his treachery.

Aldo Goran sighed as he gazed out of the huge window of his apartment across the grey waters of Lac Leman. Any moment it would start snowing. He planned to spend Christmas in Rome and after that a few weeks in Morocco.

For the time being Deepwood Grange could take care of itself. All the apartments, save one, had been sold, and if the present crop of residents wanted to get out, that was their concern. It was unfortunate if their properties would no longer fetch the prices they had paid for them, but that wasn't his fault. It wasn't as if he had deliberately planned two murders just to depress values. These things happened in an untidy world.

Aldo Goran had operated in the illicit diamond business for a long while and had made a vast amount of money. Once you had mastered the ins and outs and knew who was who, it was all so much simpler than disposing of gold bars or fragile old masters.

Though many of his business interests were now legitimate, he didn't wish to lose touch with the more exciting side of his life. There was nothing in an honest deal that could equal the thrill and tingling enjoyment of a well-planned and skilfully executed criminal venture.

Once Christmas was over he would give his mind to another money-gathering operation.

Meanwhile, with snow starting to fall outside, he somewhat tensely awaited news of latest events at Deepwood Grange.

CHAPTER 21

Though central London was clear, Rosa ran into fog as soon as she reached the Kingston bypass. It had formed the previous evening and the early morning news had carried reports of flight delays and cancellations at Heathrow and Gatwick airports. It would, however, have had to be ten times worse to put Rosa off her journey to Deepwood Grange.

As soon as she had returned to her office from court, she had tried to call Margaret, but still to no avail. She had then dialled the Binfields' number. Lady Binfield had answered and, assuming that Rosa wished to speak to her husband, said that Sir Wesley had gone into Chichester to visit his dentist.

'I'm ringing about Margaret', Rosa broke in. 'I'm very worried as I've been unable to get in touch with her. Do you know if she's all right?'

'We haven't seen her since yesterday morning when news of poor Tim Moxon's death left us all stunned. Would you like me to go and knock on her door?'

'I'd be most grateful. I'll hang on.'

'Very well, I'll go straight away.'

It seemed to Rosa that she was away for ages. What on earth could she be doing? She had only to go a few yards along the gallery and she would find out soon enough if Margaret was there. Eventually, however, a breathless Lady Binfield returned to the telephone.

'I'm sorry if I've been rather a long time. But as I couldn't get any reply to my ringing and knocking I thought I'd go down to the main entrance and see if her

morning paper and letters were still in her pigeon-hole.'
She paused. 'They were, but even so I'm sure you don't
need to be too worried. She probably had to go away
suddenly and didn't have time to let you know.' She
paused again before adding in a sad voice, 'I'm afraid
everything that's happened here has tended to spoil our
once neighbourly spirit.'

That was hardly surprising, Rosa thought.

'Thank you for doing what you have, Lady Binfield',
she said. 'I'll be coming down immediately.'

'Is there anything else you'd like me to do?'

'No, thank you. I'll probably see you this afternoon.'

'Wesley will be back from the dentist and we'll both be
in. One has to go on trying to live a normal life', she said
in the same sad voice.

Ten minutes later, Rosa was on her way. Robin was
out when she left, so she explained her anxieties to
Stephanie before departing.

'How long do you expect to be away?' the ever
practical Stephanie asked.

'I could be back tonight. It all depends on events. Tell
Robin I'll call him at home.'

'Drive carefully', Stephanie said. 'There's not only fog
about, but you're in a high old state of nerves.'

Rosa smiled ruefully. 'I know.'

It was exactly half past two when she turned into the
drive of Deepwood Grange. During the journey her
thoughts had stampeded around her head. She had
seldom felt so tense with anxiety, such had been the effect
of Mickey Rogers's casually proffered item of gossip.

As the house came into view, she saw the Binfields'
Rover 2500 parked on the gravel of the forecourt. It was
the only car there. She drew up beside it, got out and
hurried toward the front door.

Please let her be in, she murmured to herself as she
pressed Margaret's bell. But the entryphone remained

mute. A moment later she tried the Binfields' bell and Sir Wesley's voice came crackling out.

'Who is it?'

'Rosa Epton.'

There was a buzz and the door clicked open. Sir Wesley was standing at the half-open door of their apartment when she reached the gallery.

'Come in', he said gruffly. 'Not that we have any news, I'm afraid. Sally told me you'd called when I returned at lunchtime. I've been down to the garages to check if Margaret's car is still there, but it's not.'

Rosa blinked in surprise. This was totally unexpected and hadn't entered her calculations at all. But perhaps it was more reassuring than otherwise. It meant that Margaret *had* gone away and wasn't lying dead in her apartment.

'I can't think where she's gone', she said with a wan smile. 'It's most mysterious.'

'I'm sure your godmother is well able to look after herself', Sir Wesley observed judicially. 'In my view it's premature to worry about her unduly, despite recent events.'

'You don't happen to know whether any of the other residents have any knowledge of her movements?' Rosa enquired with a small flicker of hope.

'You can only find that out by making door to door calls', Sir Wesley said austerely. 'My wife suggested she should make such enquiries before you arrived, but I told her not to.' He pursed his lips in a disapproving manner. 'We've reached the point where we had best keep ourselves to ourselves until the whole horrendous affair has been resolved. I've advised my wife to keep away from the other residents for the time being.'

As if they might be plague carriers, Rosa reflected. She suddenly espied Sally Binfield hovering uncertainly at the end of the hall.

'Would you like a cup of tea, dear?' Lady Binfield said as she caught Rosa's eye.

'No, thank you very much. It's kind of you, but I think I'll press on with my enquiries about Margaret. I just wish I had a key to her apartment.'

'You'll probably need the services of a locksmith', Sir Wesley said. 'Unless you enlist the help of the police, though I suspect they'd require better cause before forcing an entry.'

I can give them good cause all right, Rosa thought grimly.

'I'll let you know what I find out', she said as she turned to go.

'Please do, dear', Lady Binfield said. 'I'd be so distressed to think that anything might have happened to Margaret.'

'We'll probably see you later then', Sir Wesley said stiffly.

It was in a sombre frame of mind that Rosa made her way round the gallery to the Potters' front door. She now feared the worst, without being able to define its precise shape.

'Oh, hello, it's you', a bleary-eyed Thelma Potter said as she peered uncertainly at Rosa. Her hair looked as if she had just come out of a wind tunnel. 'You woke me up.'

'I'm so sorry', Rosa said, aware of a powerful smell of gin wafting in her direction. 'I wondered if you'd seen Margaret recently. She seems to have vanished.'

'She's not here', Thelma said aggressively.

'I wasn't suggesting that. I just wanted to find out if you'd seen her in the past twenty-four hours.'

'Last twenty-four hours', Thelma repeated vaguely as she swayed gently in front of Rosa. 'What's so special about the last twenty-four hours?'

'I spoke to her on the phone yesterday morning and

she asked me to call her in the evening, but I've not been able to get any reply, either then or today.'

'She won't be with Doug. He only likes floosies with big bosoms.'

Uncertain how to react to this observation, Rosa remained silent.

'He's gone, you know', Thelma went on.

'Gone?'

'Buggered off. It's not the first time he's done it. He just said he was sick of being questioned by the police and went.'

'I'm so sorry', Rosa said with a feeling of helplessness. 'When did he go?'

'Yesterday evening.'

'He'll probably be back soon.'

Thelma gave an indifferent shrug. 'He can have gone for good for all I care.' She focused her watery eyes on Rosa's face. 'I expect you always thought we were as happy as mating gazelles. Balls to that! Doug could be a real bastard when he wanted, which was a lot of the time, and the only reason I've stuck with him all these years is because I'm a lazy cow.' Her face seemed suddenly to collapse as tears began to trickle down her cheeks. 'I must go and have a lie down', she said, closing her eyes and leaning against the wall.

Rosa felt she should make an offer of help, but didn't know what to suggest. Moreover, she suspected that Thelma would find greater solace in the gin bottle than in anyone's ministrations.

'I hope everything will turn out all right for you', she murmured inadequately as she turned to go.

As she made her way to the ground floor she pondered Doug Potter's disappearance. She wouldn't have thought he was the sort to be upset by police questioning, but maybe that was merely an excuse to take off on another philander. Some men never grew too old for that, it seemed.

She arrived outside Alison Tremlett's door and pressed the bell.

'Hello, Rosa, I was half-expecting to see you', Alison said in a self-congratulatory tone as she opened the door.

She was wearing a long, shapeless knitted dress which reached from her shoulders to below her calves. Its colour was an unbecoming puce.

'I suppose you've come to ask about Margaret?' she went on.

'Yes, I'm worried about her. When did you last see her?'

'Yesterday evening, around seven o'clock.'

'Where was she?'

'Disappearing down the drive in her car and going as if her life depended on it.' Alison's tone was smug and triumphant.

'Have you any idea where she was going?'

'None. But she's not back, is she? Her car's still missing from its garage.'

'So I understand', Rosa said, trying not to be riled by the other's manner. 'I gather you didn't speak to her when you saw her yesterday?'

'She drove past me like an express train.'

'I can't think where she's gone', Rosa said, ignoring the note of malice in Alison's tone. 'Nobody seems to know what's happened to her.' A small frown gathered on her brow. 'Was she alone in the car when you saw her?'

'I didn't see anyone else,' Alison said. 'It was dark and I'd gone down to the village to post a letter. It was an excuse to get a breath of air as I'd been writing all afternoon. As I returned along the drive, her car passed me. If I'd not stepped quickly on to the verge I'd have been mown down.' She paused and her eyes glinted behind her spectacles. 'What with poor Tim's body being discovered in the morning and Margaret vanishing in the evening, it was a memorable day.' She seemed to be sizing Rosa up before she spoke again. 'As I said to you once before, you obviously don't know as much about your godmother as you are led to believe.'

'It definitely was her car?' Rosa said, ignoring Alison's small, spiteful thrusts.

'Certainly it was', Alison replied sharply. 'There was no mistaking it.'

'And you're quite sure Margaret was driving?'

'Absolutely sure. She was staring straight ahead of her as if she was fleeing from something.'

Rosa shook her head in bewilderment while Alison calmly observed her.

'Have you by any chance seen John and Desmond today?' Rosa asked, looking up and meeting the other's gaze.

'They're away. They went off yesterday', Alison said with an omniscient smirk. 'John's uncle has had a serious heart attack and John was called to his bedside. He's his only close relative.'

'Where does the uncle live?'

'He's in hospital in Birmingham.'

'It's a big city. Which hospital, I wonder?'

'I've no idea. Anyway, what's it matter to you?'

'It could matter a great deal', Rosa retorted, as she turned briskly on her heel and left Alison gaping at her back.

169

CHAPTER 22

As Rosa accelerated down the drive, she had the feeling that she was fleeing from a ghost town, for that was what Deepwood Grange seemed to have become in the short time she had known it.

When she arrived at the police station she was greeted by a balding and somewhat bullish detective constable whom she had met at the house on her visit following the discovery of David Anderson's body. He spotted Rosa as he passed through the enquiries office.

'It's Miss Epton, isn't it, the solicitor from London?' he said in a tone that patted itself on the back for cleverness. 'I'm DC Roche.'

'Yes, I remember we've met. You're part of Chief Inspector James's team.'

'You could put it like that', he said, making a slight face. 'Anyway, what can I do for you?'

'I'd like to have a word with Mr James as a matter of urgency.'

'He's not here at the moment. He shouldn't be long if you want to wait. Anything I can do to help?'

Rosa hadn't cared for him the first time they had met and felt no differently now.

'I've just come from Deepwood Grange,' she said, 'but the place is almost deserted. Everyone's away.'

'Everyone?'

'I'm chiefly concerned about Mrs Lakington, who has mysteriously disappeared—'

'—Are you suggesting she may have been murdered

like the other two?' he broke in.

'Please God, no! It's just that she has gone off without a word to anyone and I'm worried about her.'

'She's your aunt, isn't she?'

'My godmother, actually.'

'Same thing as far as I'm concerned. Anyway, who else has disappeared?'

'I gather Mr Dixon and Mr Murray have been called to the bedside of Mr Dixon's uncle, who's in hospital.'

DC Roche snorted. 'Sick uncles, grandmothers' funerals, they're just age-old excuses. My bet is they've gone off on a homosexual frolic. But as long as it's outside our police area I don't mind.' His tone belied the tolerance of his words. 'If you want my view, the pendulum has swung too far. Giving queers so much licence was a disastrous piece of legislation. They almost have the run of the country. Personally, I wouldn't give them free seats in an empty cinema. But you don't have to agree with me.'

'That's as well, because I don't', Rosa replied.

'I've just seen Mr James's car come into the yard', he said before Rosa was required to make any further comment. 'I'll go and tell him you're here.'

'Thank you', Rosa said with a good deal of relief.

A few minutes later she was taken to the detective chief inspector's office.

'Good afternoon, Miss Epton. I understand you wanted to see me urgently. I hope it's something that will help me wind up my enquiries.'

'You're that close to an arrest?'

'A half-turn of the right key could be all I need.' He gave her an inviting nod. 'I'm all ears, Miss Epton.'

He listened in silence while Rosa told him of Mickey Rogers's disclosure to her that morning and what she had learnt during her visit to Deepwood Grange in the course of the afternoon.

171

When she finished, he rewarded her with a satisfied smile.

'There's only one further detail I need to have', he remarked.

'What's that?' Rosa asked with a slight frown.

'The registration number of Mrs Lakington's car.'

CHAPTER 23

When Margaret regained consciousness she found herself in total darkness, and without a sound reaching her ears. Perhaps I'm dead, she thought for a moment. But then she became aware of her body. Her feet were icy cold, but her head was throbbing and she had a raging thirst. As her mind slowly came to life, she realised she was lying under a blanket, which also covered her head. She felt painfully stiff and sore in all her joints.

She discovered that her hands were tied behind her back and that her legs were pinioned at the ankles. There was also a gag in her mouth. But none of her bonds were particularly tight. It was as if her captors hadn't wanted to do more than effectively immobilise her for a period.

She gave a small wriggle and succeeded in shaking the blanket off her face. Immediately she felt cooler, even though she had given her head a painful bang against something hard. She paused to try and work out where she was. After a further wriggle she came to the conclusion that she was in the boot of a car. Presumably her own car. This was confirmed by the blanket, which had a faintly familiar smell.

Provided she had the strength, she felt that she should eventually be able to free herself. She must remain calm and conserve her energy. If she started to panic, she would only make things worse. Strength was the operative word. Though mentally tough, she was no James Bond and she already ached in every limb as if she had spent days on the rack.

So she was lying curled up in the boot of her car, trussed and covered by a blanket. But where was the car? It was certainly stationary, but where? In a car park? Outside someone's house? Or in a wood miles from anywhere? She strained her ears for any sound that might provide a clue to her whereabouts.

She recalled that she had been driving for some time when she was ordered to stop. Almost immediately something had been squirted in her face and she had lost consciousness. It had been foggy at the time and driving had been difficult on the cross-country roads.

But how long ago was all that and where was she now?

She managed to squirm into a more comfortable position, though the term was purely relative. More than ever she longed for something to drink and tortured herself with a vision of a jug of ice-cold lime juice.

If she could manage to free her hands, then she could remove the gag and untie her ankles.

But even though her hands were only loosely tied, it clearly wasn't the intention that she should free herself too easily. She began to flex her wrists, but the only result was to chafe the skin and give her a searing pain in her shoulders.

Perhaps it would be simpler just to lie there and await events. At least she could now breathe more easily with the blanket partially off her face.

The boot of her car was a roomy one and she doubted whether it was airtight, so that the prospect of slow asphyxiation didn't strike her as a reality. Somebody must surely find her before that stage was reached.

She was suddenly overwhelmed by a feeling of

173

outrage. How dare anyone treat her in this way at her age! The sense of utter indignity was as acute as the physical discomfort she was suffering. She gave an angry heave, which resulted in a violent shooting pain down her right arm. It felt as if she had wrenched it right out of its socket.

She sank back, exhausted by an effort that had achieved nothing. She closed her eyes and said a small prayer.

Quite suddenly the lid of the boot was opened and the blanket was pulled back.

'She's still out', a voice said.

'She can't be, it's been hours', said a more distant voice. 'She's probably just asleep. Better give her another squirt of gas. We don't want her waking up now.'

Margaret made one supreme effort to raise herself up and confront her tormentors, to scream oaths at them through her gag and attract the attention of anyone who might be around.

Firm hands, however, pushed her down and a moment later the world of reality was replaced by a vision of beautiful cascading colours.

CHAPTER 24

Rosa stood on the steps of the police station wondering what to do next. Chief Inspector James had promised to let her know as soon as he had news of Margaret and had suggested that she should, meanwhile, return to London. There was, he pointed out perfectly reasonably, nothing she could do by remaining in Chichester.

Nevertheless she found herself reluctant to leave the

centre of operations. She felt that by staying close to the police, she was somehow closer to Margaret. It was an instinctive rather than a rational reaction.

She was turning the possibilities over in her mind when a now familiar voice spoke at her side.

'Here we are again, Miss Epton!'

'What on earth are you doing here?' Rosa asked, with curiously mixed feelings at finding Peter Chen once more standing in her shadow.

'That's exactly what you said to me at court this morning', he said with an engaging smile. 'Let me explain. After your abrupt departure which left me standing on the pavement, I phoned Alison and she told me what had been happening at Deepwood Grange.'

'You mean about my godmother?'

'Yes, and about Dixon's and Murray's departure. My guess is that they were with Mrs Lakington.'

Rosa gave him a startled look.

'Alison said Margaret was alone in her car.'

'The other two could have been keeping their heads down. I don't imagine they'd have wanted to be spotted until well away from the house.'

'But where was she driving them?'

'An airport, would you think?' he enquired with one eyebrow quizzically raised.

'I gather there've been almost no flights out of Heathrow or Gatwick for the past twenty-four hours.'

'Which means we still have a chance.'

'A chance?'

'To find them before they leave the country.'

Rosa glanced at him suspiciously.

'Are you being serious?'

'Yes. Most serious. You see, I have a very good idea where they may be.'

'Where?'

'Let's get in my car and be on our way. Time is

175

important.'

Rosa followed him across to his parked BMW, wondering why she had trust in him. After all, what did she really know about this soft spoken, half-Chinese solicitor who kept popping up unexpectedly? The answer was precious little, and yet it never occurred to her that she might be walking into a trap.

'Where are we going?' she asked, as they left Chichester behind and were on the road to Arundel and Brighton.

'To a village called Mulley Green. It's only a few miles from Gatwick.'

'And what happens at Mulley Green?'

'Dixon and Murray have a small house there. It's called Rose Cottage of all corny names. Provided flights don't get back to normal within the next few hours, I think we may find our friends there.'

'How do you know all this?'

'Since David's death, I've spent hour after hour going through his papers. I was determined to find out who killed him and ensure they were punished. Unfortunately, they had ample opportunity to destroy most of the evidence, but I found a tape hidden in a secret drawer of David's desk at Deepwood Grange which they hadn't discovered. . . .'

'Are we still talking about John Dixon and Desmond Murray?'

'Yes. They killed David because they found him planting a listening device in the unoccupied apartment next to theirs and realised he was on their track. It's the only explanation. My guess is that they hid his body up the chimney intending to retrieve it later and dispose of it at their convenience. But along came the men the next day or so and sealed the fireplace, only to unseal it again a week later when the people moving in decided they wanted an open gas fire put in.' He paused. 'Tim Moxon had let David have a key to the empty apartment and, of course, once he was rumbled as a friend and collaborator of David, his own life was in danger. They couldn't be sure how much he knew or might tell. Knowing how close to his chest David always played his hand, I suspect poor Tim knew very little, whatever he may have suspected.'

'Dixon and Murray must also have had a key to the unoccupied apartment', Rosa said, thoughtfully. 'I think I can guess where it came from.'

'Aldo Goran?'

'Yes. He probably kept keys to every door in the house.'

'Do you know the true identities of John Dixon and Desmond Murray?' Peter Chen asked.

'Yes.'

'Is that what Mickey Rogers told you this morning?'

Rosa gave him a sharp, questioning glance.

'How did you guess?'

'Your reaction when he spoke to you. I was watching. There was he looking as pleased as a sandfly and you with a pole-axed expression. And the way you then dashed off, I realised something was up.'

'I must obviously practise a bit of oriental inscrutability', Rosa remarked drily. She went on, 'I still think it was a thoroughly cunning move on their part. Who'd ever suspect a couple of gay young men of having been involved in a diamond robbery? In fact, they're brothers, Gordon and Gary Shipton, and from what Mickey said no more gay than Henry the Eighth.' She was thoughtful for a moment. 'The funny thing is that almost the first time I met them, I remember thinking their voices were not unalike when they used certain words. It was a matter of inflection, but I never gave it further thought and later couldn't even recall what it was that had struck me about them. It was when Margaret and I were

177

having morning coffee with them in Chichester that I registered the impression – except that I didn't register it at all. It was immediately consigned to my subconscious.'

'I told you that if we pooled our resources, we'd solve the case', Chen said confidently.

'Have you already been to Rose Cottage?' Rosa asked.

'I've looked it over.'

'I suppose they thought a hideout near to an airport would be a useful acquisition.'

'Especially if you're in the quick getaway business.'

Rosa was silent for a while. 'Do you think we ought to have let the police in on this?'

'Let's first see what we find', he said. 'You're not frightened, are you?'

'I'll tell you later.'

They drove on in silence, each absorbed in their own thoughts. Rosa's mind dwelt on Margaret and all the things that might have happened to her. Peter Chen, for his part, concentrated his thinking on the couple who had killed his friend, whose death he was determined to avenge.

Almost an hour went by before he said, 'We're nearly there.' Then a few minutes later he added, 'We'll park here. It's only a hundred yards down the road and we'd best walk the rest of the way.'

Rosa glanced at her watch as she got out of the car. It was only just after six o'clock, though it seemed that whole days must have passed since she got up that morning.

The fog had largely lifted and even as they began walking a plane roared overhead, its lights reflected mistily through the murk.

It was a street of haphazard houses which gave the impression of having been dumped at irregular intervals along the way.

'It's the next one', Peter Chen said. 'There's a track running up the far side into a yard at the back, which'll be our best approach.'

Rosa peered over a hedge at the front of the house, which appeared to be in darkness. There was a small garden that managed to give an impression of unkempt-ness.

'Give me your hand', Chen said, as they turned up the track, and Rosa unhesitatingly did so. The track was rough and she stumbled a couple of times.

By the time they drew level with the rear of the house, her eyes had become accustomed to the dark.

Light shone through a drawn blind over what, Rosa assumed, was the kitchen window. Suddenly the dis-torted image of a man's figure was reflected against the blind and Chen let out a satisfied sigh.

Rosa, meanwhile, was staring across the yard to where a car was parked beneath an open-sided, corrugated-iron shed. Her heart leapt as she recognised the contours of Margaret's Mercedes. It was facing outwards for a quick departure. She let go of Peter Chen's hand and hurried toward it.

To her surprise the driver's door wasn't locked, but there was nobody inside the car. She moved round to the back which was right up against the rear of the shed. The boot was unlatched and the lid was open a couple of inches.

As she lifted it, a bundle of blankets on the floor of the boot suddenly gave a convulsive heave. She tore them away and let out a sob as she saw Margaret lying there.

'Oh, God!' she muttered through clenched teeth, as she sought feverishly to remove the gag.

She cradled Margaret's head in her arms, though not before her godmother had let out a piercing scream.

'It's me, Rosa', she said in an urgent tone. 'You'll be all right now, but we have to be absolutely quiet.'

179

Margaret stared at her disbelievingly and, at the same time, Rosa heard shouting from the direction of the house.

This was followed by further shouts and a number of terrifying thuds, interspersed with ferocious grunts. Then, suddenly, there was total silence.

'Are you all right, Rosa?' Peter Chen asked, materialising at her side.

'Yes. Can you help me free Margaret? What's happened?'

'Your godmother's scream brought them running out', he said in a voice that betrayed no emotion. 'I was able to deal with each in turn.'

Rosa stared at him in bemusement. 'Deal with them? What have you done to them?'

'I'm an expert in karate', he said demurely. 'It wasn't difficult. They came out separately like the lambs to the slaughter.'

'You mean you've killed them?' Rosa said, aghast.

'I decided not to', he replied, as though the decision had been touch and go. 'They are merely incapacitated. Here, let me carry Mrs Lakington indoors and we'll phone the police.'

Gordon and Gary Shipton, or John and Desmond as Rosa still thought of them, lay sprawled outside the back door like battlefield casualties.

Rosa stepped over their inert bodies with eyes averted.

CHAPTER 25

It took all Rosa's and a doctor's efforts to persuade
Margaret to go to hospital.

'I won't be responsible for the consequences if you
refuse', the doctor said. 'There's every likelihood that
you'll be able to go home tomorrow, but it's essential you
stay in overnight for various tests.'

Rosa went with her in the ambulance, sitting beside
the stretcher and holding her godmother's hand.

'The worst part has been the disillusionment', Margaret said in a voice more hoarse than usual. 'I still can't
help liking them. They were always so much more fun
than the rest of the residents.'

'That's being very charitable, seeing how they treated
you', Rosa remarked.

'They could have treated me much worse. After all,
they could have put a plastic bag over my head. And
when we reached that final place – Rose Cottage, did you
say? – they left the lid of the boot open to give me more
air. And brought me something to drink.'

'Don't romanticise them! They're murderers', Rosa
said sternly.

'Do you know what Desmond said about you?'
Margaret went on. 'That he regretted having to pretend
he was gay as he rather fancied you.'

'The cool cheek', Rosa said, aware, however, of a
sudden responsive twitch within her. 'How did they
persuade you to drive them?'

'They asked me down for a drink yesterday evening. I
knew you were going to phone me, but imagined, of

course, that I'd be back in time. I'd been there about half an hour when John suddenly left the room. On his return he asked if I would drive them to Chichester Station. Their own car was out of action, he said, and they had to dash off to visit a dying uncle in hospital. Naturally, I said I would, and added that I'd go back to my own apartment to get ready and return in about twenty minutes. John asked me if I had my car keys in my bag and when I said that I had, he told me to stay in their apartment until they were ready. Even then I didn't really suspect anything, though I was a bit surprised by his sudden change of manner. Then, a few minutes later, Desmond calmly produced a revolver and pointed it at me. It was then various pennies started to drop. They made me walk ahead of them as we went to the garage. Once we'd got into the car, they kept right down out of sight at the back, but I was reminded that the revolver was aimed at the base of my spine. I set off down the drive like a bat out of hell.'

'Did they say where they wanted you to take them?'

'No. I realised, of course, it wasn't the railway station. They just told me to take the Brighton road, but after about ten miles, they directed me on to side roads. It wasn't long after that they ordered me to stop the car and I was knocked out with some gas spray. When I came to, the car was stationary. I've been thinking about where that could have been and have concluded it was probably one of the airport car parks. Later, they returned to the car, presumably because there were still no planes flying, and I was given another dose of gas. When I next came to, the car was bumping all over the place and then it came to a halt. Desmond opened the boot and peered at me with a torch and I indicated that if I didn't have more air, I'd die, so he left the lid open a fraction after making sure I was still properly gagged and tied up.' She paused. 'I'm still not clear why they couldn't have used their own car, as I don't imagine it was really out of action.'

'I suspect they thought the police might well be on the look-out for their car at some stage or another whereas yours would pass unnoticed. After all, they obviously left in a great hurry and presumably weren't sure how much time they had to make good their escape. The discovery of Tim Moxon's body yesterday morning plainly had a catalysing effect.'

'Was it really only yesterday morning? It seems like a lifetime ago.'

When the ambulance reached the hospital, Rosa gave the people in charge of the casualty department the particulars of Margaret that they required. It seemed that the doctor who had attended her at Rose Cottage had already phoned ahead, so that little time was lost in admitting her.

'I'll be back later', Rosa said. 'And tomorrow, all being well, I'll be able to take you home.'

'Where are you going now?'

'Back to Rose Cottage. I'll get a taxi.'

'You will come down for Christmas, won't you.' Margaret said drowsily as they wheeled her away.

As Rosa left the hospital, a police car pulled up outside and two officers, whom she recognised, hurried in. She was relieved that they didn't appear to notice her.

On her return to Rose Cottage, she found the yard full of cars and police officers. On identifying herself, however, she was allowed to enter the house.

Peter Chen was sitting on a chair in the kitchen, looking his most inscrutable, while Detective Chief Inspector James paced up and down in front of him, looking distinctly savage.

'Ah!' he exclaimed, as Rosa came into the room. 'Is Mrs Lakington all right?'

'Fine, considering what she's been through. I'm sure

she'll be as right as rain after a good night's rest.'

'She's a tough lady.' Then, fixing Rosa with a hard look, he went on, 'I've been telling Mr Chen that what he and you did was extremely stupid and could have placed innocent lives at risk. I'm surprised that two members of the legal profession could have behaved so irresponsibly.'

'Are you referring to our having caught two murderers for you?' Rosa asked, stung by his tone.

'I'm referring to your unwarranted meddling in a police matter.'

'If we hadn't meddled, as you put it, the odds are that the Shiptons would have left the country before you could do anything about it. What's more, my godmother could easily have become their third victim.'

'It was your duty to pass your information on to the police, not embark on personal heroics.'

'There was nothing heroic in what I did', Rosa retorted. 'And anyway, we were going to inform you as soon as we'd confirmed they were here.'

'That's right, Chief Inspector', Chen broke in. 'Had it not been for Mrs Lakington's scream alerting them, that's what we'd have done.'

James stared from one to the other, apparently wrestling with a cross-current of emotions.

'I must say, Mr Chen,' he said at length, 'that I've never before had two wanted men served up to me quite so oven-ready.' Chen gave a small bow and James went on, 'Do you realise that one way and another this case has involved almost half the residents of Deepwood Grange?' He paused. 'And to think that when I began my enquiries, it was what turns out to be the uninvolved half of whom I was most suspicious.' He shook his head in a rueful manner. 'After all, there was one murderer already in residence, though I know I shouldn't say that in view of the jury's verdict. As for the lady who writes up-market porn, she'd be capable of anything in her nutty way. Incidentally, I have no doubt that it was one of the Shiptons who banged her over the head that night. I imagine she'd been over in Moxon's apartment on a bedtime visit and came tripping back just as the Shiptons were getting ready to pay what was to be their final visit on him. She probably heard some sound or other and was knocked out to dampen her curiosity.' For the first time that evening he smiled. 'Anyway, thanks. And now I'd better go and arrange for our pair of pseudo gays to be taken back and charged. By the time we've finished with them, they'll be facing quite a lot of charges.'

After he had left the room, Rosa let out a heavy sigh.

Peter Chen looked thoughtful for a while. Then he said, 'I think David would be pleased. Not so much that his death has been avenged, as that we've managed to finish off what he began.' He glanced round the small, cheerless kitchen, before turning back to Rosa. 'Do you like Chinese food, Rosa?'

'On occasions.'

'Might you be able to enjoy a really good Chinese dinner once a fortnight or so?'

'I think that's very possible', Rosa replied with a particularly warm smile.

>>> If you've enjoyed this book and would like to discover more great vintage crime and thriller titles, as well as the most exciting crime and thriller authors writing today, visit: >>>

The Murder Room
Where Criminal Minds Meet

themurderroom.com